ELEY WILLIAMS is an author of novels and short stories. Her debut collection of fiction *Attrib. and Other Stories* (2017) was awarded the Republic of Consciousness Prize and the James Tait Black Memorial Prize and was longlisted for the 2018 Dylan Thomas Prize. Her novel *The Liar's Dictionary* won a 2021 Betty Trask Award, was shortlisted for the Desmond Elliott Prize and was listed as a *Guardian* Book of the Year. In 2023, she was selected as one of *Granta*'s Best of Young British Novelists. Her writing is published in journals and anthologies including *Modern Queer Poets*, *The Penguin Book of the Contemporary British Short Story* and *Liberating the Canon*, with stories and serialised fiction also commissioned by Radio 4. She is a Fellow of the Royal Society of Literature.

Praise for *Attrib.*:

'She is a writer for whom one struggles to find comparison, because she has arrived in a class of her own: witty, melancholy, occasionally sensual, occasionally mordant, elegantly droll without the kind of hipster quirkiness that makes me want to hurl books at the wall. She has in common with George Saunders the ability to be both playful and profound, and we are lucky to have her'

SARAH PERRY,

'It's just the real inexplicable gorgeous brilliant thing this book. I love it in a way I usually reserve for people'

MAX PORTER, author of *Grief Is The Thing With Feathers*

'I came late to Eley Williams and am happy to have found her. Hearing her read her short story "Smote" aloud recently blew me away'

DAISY JOHNSON, author of *Everything Under*

'Funny, playful and utterly bravura, it deserves to be read by everyone with a love of words and an interest in the way deftly wielded language and original ideas can come together to detonate on the page … a seam of deep feeling runs through most of the stories, and they're leavened with the kind of deft, unexpected humour that had me grinning broadly on a packed train and at one point emitting a surprised honk of mirth'

MELISSA HARRISON, author of *All Among the Barley*, in the *Financial Times*

'In the aftermath of *Attrib. and Other Stories* by Eley Williams, I had to resist the urge to weigh every book in my house in order to find the heaviest'

SARA BAUME, author of *A Line Made By Walking*, in *New Statesman* Books of the Year

'It's exciting to come across a writer playing with language so experimentally. There's no one working in the UK quite like her'

JOANNA WALSH, author of *Worlds from the Word's End*

'A joyous collection of moments, of love, of language, with such a light, skilled touch'

ALIYA WHITELEY, author of *The Beauty*

'*Attrib. and Other Stories* cornered the market in cerebral playfulness' *Guardian*, Best Books of the Year

'It's exhilarating to dive into the associative rush of Williams' writing' *Vanity Fair*

'It proved you can generate acrobatic, edge-of-your-seat fiction from little more than random arcana' *Telegraph*

'An emotionally delicate and tenderly introspective collection' *New Statesman*

‘It is impossible not to identify with Williams’ candid observations of the quirks and quandaries of emotional life. Her experimentation is not a case of obfuscation: we come away feeling that we know precisely what she means ... Wondrous things, shots of linguistic pleasure that take moments of everyday life and fashion something marvellous from them’ *Times Literary Supplement*

‘The letters in her words seemed to be drawn from adjacent parts of the alphabet. They had thought about themselves and one another. There was something collusive about them. They backed up one another’s story. They had demanded to be consulted, and come to their own unconventional arrangements. It all makes for alphabetophile writing. In the reader, it produces a kind of constructive estrangement from words. Think William Gass, Lydia Davis or Anne Carson, and you won’t be too wrong’

MICHAEL HOFMANN, *London Review of Books*

‘Fiddling with words, as if playing with them were all that mattered, her characters draw time to a standstill – then they stop, suddenly, blinking and thrilled. It’s beautiful, the way they get lost’ *Guardian*

‘No fiction writer was more exciting on sentence level’

The White Review

‘Williams’ writerly roots in poetry and poetic prose shine throughout this stunning collection of almost intimidatingly intelligent and creative work’ *Mslexia Magazine*

‘An absolute must-read for anyone remotely interested in the contemporary short story’ *The London Magazine*

‘The possibilities these stories imply are many, one of them being that you, the reader, could be their unnamed narrator. That’s why, like all good literature, they feel so personal, immediate and incredibly urgent’ *New Humanist*

‘So good it makes me giddy. For God’s sake, buy a copy’

Caught by the River

‘Williams’ USP (even, at times, brilliance), is to drop us in on lives at seemingly innocuous moments – and then wrong foot the reader, contort the unfolding story, and ultimately distil something elemental from the seemingly banal’

3:AM Magazine

'Fixates on the briefest moments of confusion and miscommunication – the kind of exchanges that feel so vivid, but look so mundane from the outside ... Williams brings these moments of internal intensity into the spotlight, with 170 pages that positively glow' *Fader Magazine*

'Williams' entertaining and versatile first collection must be attributed – or "yield[ed] as due" – the resounding praise it deserves' *Review 31*

Attrib.
and Other Stories

ALSO BY ELEY WILLIAMS

The Liar's Dictionary

Moderate to Poor, Occasionally Good

Attrib. and Other Stories

Eley Williams

4th ESTATE • *London*

4th Estate
An imprint of HarperCollins*Publishers*
1 London Bridge Street
London SE1 9GF

www.4thEstate.co.uk

HarperCollins*Publishers*
Macken House, 39/40 Mayor Street Upper
Dublin 1, D01 C9W8, Ireland

First published in Great Britain in 2017 by Influx Press
This 4th Estate paperback edition published in 2024

1

A catalogue record for this book is
available from the British Library

ISBN 978-0-00-870872-6

Set in Stempel Garamond LT Std
Printed and bound in the UK using 100%
renewable electricity at CPI Group (UK) Ltd

for my parents

To ATTRIBUTE. *v. a.*
To aſcribe; to give; to yield as due.
To impute, as to a cauſe.

TROLMYDAMES. *n. ſ.*
[Of this word I know not the meaning.]

– Dr. Johnson's *A Dictionary of the English Language* (1755)

Contents

The Alphabet

(or Love Letters or Writing Love Letters, Before I Forget How To Use Them or These Miserable Loops Look So Much Better On Paper Than In Practice)

The plot of this is not and will not be obvious. I'm pretending that this is not important. It is quite likely that I have lost it anyway. The plot. Related – where are my glasses? For some reason I find that if I say,

'Glasses. Glasses?'

in an authoritative way while searching for them it seems more likely that I shall find them or that I will somchow *invoke them into being*. This is a strategy that does not work for finding one's dignity nor for finding you but *glasses* – possibly. Announcing my intention to find them at least conveys a sense of control as I dither around picking up ornaments and looking under curtains. There is a paper published online that sets out this thesis, and I shall quote it aloud to make it real: speech can alter 'ongoing cognitive (and even perceptual) processing in nontrivial ways' effectively allowing one to concentrate better. *Say it ain't so* – announce, with an ounce of courage and conviction and the world's your –

your –

the world's yours for the mistaking.

For what it's worth, concentrating, I can say that you altered me in non-trivial ways.

The pursuit was anything but trivial, at least. I remember that.

'Glasses?'

I completely lost it (the plot, not the glasses – they're only mislaid) about two weeks ago around the same time that I mislaid you. If you were here you would make a filthy joke about my use of that word, about you being *miss laid*. Scratch that, then. Screw it or unscrew that word out of place. Two weeks ago is when I lost it – the plot – round about the same time that you were not *mislaid* by me but were *misplaced*. When you misplaced me. Two weeks ago is when we ceased to converge by the bedside table, beneath the sofa, by the fridge.

* * *

I have realised with some embarrassment that the reason I could not find them is of course because I am *wearing* my glasses. This is like that time someone (I am being coy – I mean you) complemented no complimented my eyes and suddenly I wished that I could pop them out onto your palm and say, 'Hey, damn right, they're the best thing about me; *not, you know, functionally, of course, hence the glasses, but in terms of form*; want to swap? I wanna see you in 'em', which would of course be impossible for three reasons and horrible for about twelve, but

– *what was I saying?* –

even though I now know the whereabouts of my glasses the feeling of lack remains. I have lost something else so here I must remain, poised to retrieve. If I say,

'Something else. Something else?' in an authoritative way perhaps it is more likely that I will find it, whatever it might be.

We looked up my condition after coming home from the doctor's the first time where it had been explained to us in a pale room with a ticking light. We had looked the word up in the dictionary. I did not tell you, but I had imagined using my plucked-out eye's optic nerve as a bookmark to save the definition's place. We also searched online to make sure that our Internet history was keeping up with our life events. I spelt the word with an *f* at first and, sighing, you took control of the keyboard.

A P H A S I A, you typed. It required both of your hands in the same way that origami might or the act of unwrapping a parcel. We browsed. *Aphasia*: a disturbance of the comprehension and formulation of language caused by dysfunction in specific brain regions.

'You can't spell *aphrodisiac* without *aphasia*,' you said later, trying to make a filthy joke out of it and holding me.

'Yes you can,' I said into your jumper after a while. This gave me time to work it out.

'Well, *I* can't,' you had said, not letting go.

And I, not giving up, had said, 'You'd have a spare *A*.'

And 'Gimme me an *A*!' you had said in your cheerleader voice. I cannot remember what happened next. I probably did give you something. After all, your innuendo-led ears would probably not let me get away without *giving you one* but it is impossible to recall. I have forgotten, basically, and now I have misplaced you.

I have swept so many words under my tongue and out of the porches of my ear, out of sight and out of mind. Over the years your ears must have become spoked and fairly bristling with my *X*s and *K*s and *T*s and teasing.

* * *

The *plot*, yes – the condition of its *being lost*. I have a great deal of nostalgia for having the plot and a full vocabulary. Both have been lost gradually, along with the – *what is it* – marbles. *My* marbles, specifically. We have come to specific marbles. I have lost *it*, I have lost *my marbles* and I have lost *the plot* – the Holy Trinity of losing I have lost my faith in – wham bam thank you m' – ma – mate. Maybe the *plot* was connected with my *marbles* in some way. Maybe one plays marbles on a plot, *plot* being synonymous with *pitch* or *field* or *court*. I lost them all long ago is what's important. Two weeks ago. You took my *marbles* and *it* with you and I appear to have mislaid *the plot*. In the film-of-the-musical-of-the-play, in Hertford Hereford and Hampshire Hurricanes Hardly Ever Happened but Eliza Doolittle was fed marbles in order to improve her diction not to lose a good thing she had going, and no doubt if you were here you would make a dirty joke about that word too. I shall shun diction, then; a cunning stunt. Spoonerisms, tongue-twisters – I remember that you could make those words affectionate and filthy as soon as you found them and me in close confines.

One cannot spell *eyes* without having to also spell *yes*. This was always especially the case with you, and with yours. Incidentally, my dictionary is definitely getting smaller. This might be because I am moving away from it or because it is shrivelling.

'What's your favourite word?' you asked me on our first date.

I said something obvious like *pamphlet*.

'Excellent,' you had said. You may have even clapped. 'Favourite letter?' you continued without offering your own answer. You tended to take charge like that. A waiter was sizing-up our shoes, and handing you the bill.

I was trying to seem interesting, so I replied, *Q*.

'*Q*?' you echoed, somewhat accusingly, as you pressed your PIN code into the machine.

Yes.

'*Q* needs *U* to be useful,' you had said, and I remember that I rolled my eyes out of my head and you winked in a pantomime way and touched my wrist with your hand.

'And yours?' I think I asked. I must have done. I should have. I hope I did.

'I consider favourite letters to be a better indicator of personality than star signs,' you had said, and I had thought, *oh great this person's a massive weirdo and is going to try and inculcate me into a reiki-practising cheese-cloth-wearing bewhiskered cult or sect*, because I used to use words like *inculcate* without thinking twice even though I knew at the time that it was unadvised. Inadvised. *But by God you were charming*, said the other half of my brain. *Cult leaders often are*, replied the first half. *GO ATROPHY ON A STALK*, said the second half, and it did, I think.

Thank goodness. You had evaded my question, I couldn't help but notice.

'*A* is a snapped Eiffel Tower. The shape of it. If you were interested in *A* as a letter I'd assume that you were only interested in half-finishing projects,' you said.

'Is that right?'

'*H* is for rugby fans, and penalties. *F* and *E* and *Y* are all prongs.'

And prongs are for stabbing at something, I thought: letters as stabs in the dark. I do not know why you picked these letters as examples. You were misspelling the alphabet.

'What does *Q* imply?'

You had cocked your head as if the answer might slide out of your ear on to the table. 'Upper case or lower case?' you asked, gravely.

'That would be telling,' I said, pretending that I knew how to flirt.

'It stands for questions, often, doesn't it?' you said and I'm sure that I did not know how to answer. We went to a bar.

'*Q* was your first answer,' you said very close to my face. You were slightly drunk by this point and enjoying the sound of your own voice. I was enjoying the sound of your own voice too. 'Queuing, *lining them up*. Very British. *Q* is the old man in James Bond,' you went on. 'No, the new young man, the lovely whippety one. *Q* is for questions,' you said again, and then you had said something about liking a challenge.

And four years later after the diagnosis you were putting posters and printouts up around our flat, posters and labels. *This is a kettle* on the kettle, *these are mousetraps* on the mousetraps, *I am your one and only, and this joke only works because of a song you like* on a badge that you wore around the place.

I have a children's laminated alphabet poster on my wall. There is a cartoon apple on it, and a ball, and a large yellow cat. The grossly stunted Eiffel Tower shape of *A*, the headless, limbless woman's body of *B*; *C*'s upset urn and the taut bow of *D*; the snapped trident-head of *E* further-snapped to form an *F*. An empty workman's clamp: *G*. The rugby goal of *H*. There I am next to it, standing tall like something at stake – the following long shadow cast by the *I* some time past noon makes the *J*. What is next? *K* is the point of an arrow smacking into a trunk, while *L* is a candle-holder where the flame has been snuffed out. *M* and *N* are always claimed by my memory of your knuckles and *O* invariably is your surprise, or your singing unabashed in our garden when you think that no one is at home. Remaining in the garden the letter *P* is cuckoo-spit on the length of a chive, cooling in the dew-dawn. *Q* is a monocle, discarded. We always had time for eccentricity – we watched a battered

VHS of *My Fair Lady* and drank whenever a word game presented itself. *R* is a thrown magnifying glass embedded in a wall. To say that *S* is a snake is perhaps easy-pickings but true: my occasional lisp a snake-in-the-grass. I lisp when hurried or under stress. What's the evolutionary point in that. I resent the *S* especially. Atlas seen cruciform from the front, the world removed from his shoulders: *T*. Then *U* comes as a grin, grossly extended, or an empty jar – if there were forty we would be ready for fairyland thieves, and because you ruin things with beautiful practicality let's line up an amphora with the lip smashed clean away by vandals: *V*. Two such amphorae: *W*. The next letter marks the spot, a kiss or something like the waiter's brace-suspenders against his fresh white shirt-back: *X*. Pentecostal or horrified up-thrust arms in *Y* as we finally discover the serpent *Z*: a cruel child has broken the spine of an *S*.

Lying in bed and looking at the ceiling, I think that there can be no time for yellow cats, or balls, or apples when there is all this to remember and bear in mind.

Aphasia is now an autocomplete on my laptop's search field.

'Good thing there's a word for it,' you had said, and my face was in your jumper again.

To fill the empty kitchen, I turn to things like radios. Love songs will try and make you believe that one word is the hardest, and that three particular words are the most important – and I'm sure that those three will be the last to leave me. In truth it is impossible to place a bet on which word will be the next to go. At least I think it will be nothing to do with scansion or prosody. Perhaps it is all to do with the way a mouth moves. That your mouth moved in the kitchen, and that I can remember this clearly – that one's speaking mouth can be form over function as each word that I can remember peels away, or falls away, or does whatever you would like to call it.

'What's your favourite letter?' you had asked me, four years after the last time, the first time, when we were sitting in bed reading the Sunday papers as if I still knew how that worked.

Oh! I said.

'*O*?' you repeated.

No, emm – '*M*?'

No, I –

'*I*?' you had said and then you reached over and pressed my nose to let me know that you were only teasing.

I think that I clicked my fingers in irritation and said, 'I'll get it eventually,' and you had said, 'Oi oi, you can bet you will get it eventually,' because you cannot help yourself, your filthiness, and I had said,

'That's not funny,' and you said,

'You don't know what funny means any more,' and you

looked at me, knowing or hoping that I would laugh, and I did.

And

– you should never start sentences like that, I know,
but what's a sentence, really, if not time spent alone –

the medical pamphlets do not state it and the literature does not concentrate on it but the only two things that I have ever been scared to lose are you and – more so, and originally – my mind. There we have it! The day that I forgot the word for a hairbrush was when you first looked concerned. I held the hairbrush in front of me and trialled *scalp-tufter* after a few seconds of concentration. You had frowned.

You had cocked your head in the way that you do. And from then on it became – like *easier* but the opposite. Forgetting *hairbrush* became forgetting our address became forgetting dates became figmenting became fragmenting, became I remembered your beautiful, beautiful face but could not quite place it. My brain had unpinned you without me wanting it to and now you have gone. It is not your fault, or whatever the word is.

* * *

The heaviest book in the house is the dictionary. I know because to fill my days I went around with a scale and measured each one to learn the weight of words. The dictionary is so heavy that my hand hurts even if I brace myself when I take it down from its shelf. You used to press flowers between its pages. I didn't know that at the time, or if I did I overlooked it – but I do not think I would have overlooked such a thing. The petals that I find do not smell of anything in particular. They are brittle. The word *friable* comes to mind and I look it up at once. The new-to-me-petals fall out occasionally into my lap when I'm checking myself or checking up on myself – today there are just five that fall from the pages, three on my leg and two on the floor. They are your delicate dirty jokes I found increasingly hard to understand. I can only imagine that their colour has not changed since the time you placed them there.

As I say, the dictionary seems smaller in my hands but somehow grows heavier even as my speech-bubbles grow thinner and more gauzy above my head. I want to be able to tell you that the petals are as light-heavy as full stops. I want to be able to tell you that I miss you, and the way you had with me, and the way you had with all the words that – at the time – I had for you.

Swatch

Peter noticed the unspeakable colour during Stuart's twelfth birthday party. The house was erupting with all the usual paroxysms that accompany excellent games of Hide and Seek. There was shrieking, stomping, hissed invectives and sharply slammed doors. Peter and Stuart had happened upon the same bolthole at the very same second and they eyed each other warily on its threshold. There was no point wasting time negotiating terms or rights of way – they bundled into the airing cupboard on the upstairs landing and pushed the door shut by falling against it in a shushing, adrenalised heap.

In the airing cupboard Peter and Stuart could hear bellows of triumph and dismay through the door for the first few minutes, and partygoers' footsteps came as occasional thunder in the corridor. Each time this happened both boys covered their own mouths as if aware that some involuntary primal mechanism might prompt them to give an answering call and reveal their whereabouts. All returned to quiet soon. A triumph! They celebrated their success with hushed giggles and congratulatory dips of the elbows into each other's ribs.

These nudges gradually changed and became tangled, bored tussles for space when it became more obvious that their spot had been chosen perhaps rather too well. It occurred to Peter that they had unwittingly committed to a whole new way of life. They had already endured sharing this airing cupboard for at least thirty years or possibly a whole half an hour and the initial giddy fear of possible discovery was transforming into horrified suspicion that they might never be found again.

Stuart was not like Peter, and the birthday boy decided that he must put their cloistered time to good use. He produced a bag from his corduroy dungarees and with a solemn expression began demonstrating the best way to fit handfuls of marshmallows into Peter's mouth without causing suffocation.

'Five – six –' Stuart counted in whispered tones.

Peter crouched a little tighter with his back against the water-heater. His legs were beginning to go to sleep, but the twinge of incoming pins and needles and the discomfort of the heater's scald-creep-bloom across his back did not feel entirely bad. Peter was wearing his very favourite jumper – *Hawaiian Blue 4* cotton that featured a *Volcanic Red* alien vinyl decal giving a thumbs-up – and the water-heater made the airing cupboard smell like tinned peaches. Stuart had been hitting the jelly and ice-cream table pretty hard since breakfast and his pupils were larger than usual. As he let marshmallow upon marshmallow push past his teeth, Peter was aware that he was looking at his friend's eyes rather than looking into them, and that realising this meant that he had to look away at once. He concentrated on a knot in the wooden shelf above him for a second then felt his gaze slip back down.

Peter knew that his own eyes were an odd mix of colours. When asked for their colour he would say, 'Brown!' but not only were there odd squiggles, quirks and dots within the colours there, soft twisted braids and paisley patterns in the meat of his iris, but the actual shades of Peter's eyes changed minutely, but crucially, according to both the season and the time of day. He saw *Cocoa Latte* in his eyes some days, *Truffle Leather 3* during others. There was even a greenish contour of *Enchanted Eden 2* to be found if he examined his eye in strong morning light. Some years ago Peter really, *really* leaned in against the bathroom mirror to work out what was going on there, straining on tiptoe above the sink and making sure that he did not knock over his dad's shaving cream or contact lens fluid. In this position, if Peter stared himself down in bright summer sun he could see a notch of *Tangiers Flame* in one of his eyes and the shadow of a shadow of *Amethyst Falls* right beside it. At this discovery Peter had not been at all sure that he liked the fact that infinite variety was playing out in his face – in a way that was so plain for all to see! He burst into tears and his eyes grew hot and the blue and orange there became more vibrant: *Cerulean* shot through with *Scorched Topaz*. He had to stay in the bathroom with his head to the cool tiling for a good while before he felt brave enough to unlock the door and leave.

He had mentioned the colours in his eye to his dad at bedtime that evening and made sure not to let fear edge into his voice.

'You have hazel eyes,' said his father. He was still wearing overalls and had speckles of dried paint above his eyebrow. 'But the orange and the blue,' Peter pressed and his father turned on the bedside lamp to examine Peter's eyes very carefully, tutting and tsking, then gave a professional's nod. 'Mud and milfoil,' Peter's father said finally. 'Pondweed and a fast, peaty, strong-flowing river – that's what I see. But, you know, would you believe it? There are occasional kingfishers along the bank.' He let Peter sit up a touch in bed. He smelt of calico dustsheets and turpentine, Peter's favourite smell in the whole world. 'Do you know what a kingfisher is?'

Peter had nodded but his father was already tapping on his phone and bringing up pictures. Peter leaned in.

'I knew that,' he said.

'Have you heard the word *glaiks* before?' asked his dad.

He let Peter look it up on the phone. '"Chiefly Scots",' Peter read there. 'Go on.'

Peter hesitated, his eyes close to the phone's screen. '"*Deri* – no – der-i-sive deception, or mockery",' Peter read.

The paint on his father's eyebrow had lowered at this, and Peter let him take the phone back and scroll a little.

'This,' he pointed, 'is the one I meant. This is the meaning I meant, I mean.'

'Under the number two?'

'That's it.'

'"Chiefly Scottish",' Peter said.

'Go on.'

'"Quick flashes of light",' Peter read and then he pulled his blanket up and asked if he could look once more at the pictures of kingfishers, and that night he went to sleep knowing that what was really important about the secret colours in one's eye is the fact that somebody would have to be very-very-very close in every way before they could know anything about them.

'You have to really shove them along the sides,' Stuart was saying, sternly, as he pressed another marshmallow into Peter's mouth with his thumb. Stuart was training all his attention on the task at hand. Efficiency was not the only consideration with the current procedure and as Stuart drew each marshmallow from the bag, he insisted on inspecting it with a specialist's courtesy before putting it in place alongside Peter's teeth.

Peter tried not to breathe because he had a sense that not-breathing in this circumstance might be important. He shifted against the water-heater and studied his friend's irises a little more carefully.

French Vermouth? Was that a colour name? He thought about his dad's sample paint pot pyramid in the shop window and the magic names printed on their labels that you could say aloud and cast like spells. *Atmosphere 1*? *Jade White*?

'Ryan managed fourteen,' Stuart said in a low but conversational voice, his hand dipping once again into the marshmallow bag. 'Fourteen and he could still sing the whole of the school song and you could hear every word really clearly. Even the –' and Peter watched Stuart's eyelids narrow as he sought the right word '– the letters with the lines in them. The – the sharp ones – *ts* and things.'

Peter's throat creaked or rumbled a taut appreciative *yes*.

'*Lift! Up! Your! Hearts!*' Stuart sang quietly. As he emphasised the final glassy sibilant his wide eyes drew even wider with wonder at the memory or the imagined memory of Ryan's performance.

Peter squared his shoulders against the water-heater and gave a trial run. '*Lift! Up! Your! Hearts!*'

'*Lift!*' Stuart urged. Peter thought about the machine at

the back of his father's shop. Customers could bring in an object or a picture or a fabric or a fleck of paint that they liked and Peter's dad would pass it beneath a special lens so that the computer could run its programme and mix a combination of all its millions of potential colours. You could reproduce the exact shade you wanted and take it home with you that day sealed in a little tin. *If the surface area is half a centimetre in diameter, we can match it!* promised the poster fixed next to the machine. Peter's dad had allowed him to Blu-Tack this poster right onto the wall and in the summer holidays, when the kingfishers in Peter's eyes were at their most obvious, the Blu-Tack would swell an infinitesimal amount and the poster would sometimes slip to the floor.

'*Lift!*' Stuart repeated.

'*Lift*,' Peter said, forcefully, but the word came out all disappointing and claggy, chewy somehow and too-muffled to be much use. He saw that Stuart frowned a little as he selected another marshmallow. Peter had always hated the school song. *Above the swamps of subterfuge and shame*, all the pupils around him would shout on the first day of every term to the tune of a thudding piano, not needing to refer to their hymnals because they were so familiar with the lyrics, *The deeds, the thoughts, that honour may not name.* The whole school would swallow cubic fathoms of dusty air and announce with one voice the lines to the Assembly Hall's

Polycell-textured ceiling. *The halting tongue that dares not tell the whole!*

For whatever reason, Peter always imagined the other boys sitting next to him in their arranged ranks were all thinking about turning around to him as they sang, and that the secret skirmishing colours in their eyes would all be suddenly brighter. *Lift! Up! Your!* They would begin to pull at his blazer buttons and at his shirt. Peter could not sing this song without seeing in his mind's eye all these phantom bright-eyed boys closing in and tugging a *Brick Red* weight free from his chest. They would sing and he would fall to the parquet floor and they would raise the messy thing way above their heads in their newly *Brick Red* and glossy hands. Stuart was reaching once more for the bag, 'Thirteen –'

Both boys heard the hand fall upon the cupboard's door handle at the same time and Peter, mouth glazing over, watched his friend's extraordinary and unnameable eyes dart to the door, appalled and thrilled in equal measure.

Attrib.

I held the rib up to the microphone and opened my mouth. 'Dvorák,' said my neighbour's front door. Its pronunciation was very clear. Not quite sure who to blame for this, I narrowed my eyes at the rib.

'His and hers?' asked my computer's cooling fan.

'Lament,' said the tree branch who chose that moment to graze my windowpane, and as if in answer the hinges on our cat-flap downstairs said 'Pyongyang' in insistent tones. The fact I could hear this all the way up in my bedroom proved to be my tipping point and I pushed the printouts of the Sistine Chapel's ceiling from my lap, threw the rib to the ground and fled my desk. I wedged the swinging cat-flap shut with the second thing that came to hand (the first thing that was to hand was the cat, whose *I didn't ask to be born* look I pointedly ignored) and returned with new, incensed resolve to my computer and its waiting microphone.

I collected my pens together in a neat line along my desk-top. I collected my thoughts. I collected my breath. Feeling newly brave I picked up the shard of rib between my forefinger and thumb once more and settled back in my chair, ready for the day's work.

'Sissinghurst,' announced my radiator in its clearest tones. 'Sissinghurst and *gourds*.'

Adrenaline snarled up my spine and directly into my brain so it was in an out-of-body sleight of keyboard strokes that I set about buying soundproofing materials from the first company that I could find online. Scrolling down the page of options available to me with its unfamiliar vocabularies, I reached for my phone and dialled the number.

'Is it for a home studio?' a nice-sounding man on customer services asked.

I explained my situation and the deadlines involved. 'I cannot tolerate these conditions,' I added at the end of my speech. To fill his polite pause, I assured him that I would pay whatever figure he quoted.

'You might also want some baffles,' he said as the conversation began winding down. 'Some sound baffle panels. They'll absorb a lot.' I wrote *BAFFLE* on the back of my Sistine Chapel printout and underlined the word twice. The baffling material would arrive too late for today's purposes, of course, but at least I could make the order and pretend that I had some semblance of control. 'I've never spoken to a Foley artist before,' the man continued as we finished the order. He pronounced *Foley* as if it was the French word for madness.

'Testing testing, yes yes yes,' I said to the microphone. The neon bars on my laptop screen lit up and jittered accordingly. I messed around with the mouse and the EQ levels. 'One two, one two,' I said. Staring down into it, you can see that the grille of a microphone contains endless darknesses. 'Three,' I added. I lined up the pens in a slightly different order on my desk.

'You're – *hello*? – you're still on the line,' said a tiny voice next to my hand. I swore, apologised, hit a button and threw my phone across the room.

'Lament, lamently,' said the tree branch at my window-pane.

I picked up the rib once more and turned my attention to the printouts of the Sistine Chapel.

The commission had come from a gallery and my work for it was pretty much completed, just one task left to the last minute. The gallery was putting together an exhibition in the new year involving huge reproductions of Michelangelo's major works alongside archival material relating to his life. It was a big deal and I, a small deal, had been brought on board to add incidental sounds to the audio guides included in the ticket price. By pressing various buttons at various stages of the tour, those who wished to – and here I consult the paperwork to check that I have the right wording – *augment their experience of the paintings and statues* could access pre-recorded commentaries from art historians and have complementary pieces of music or literature or Bible verses read to them by actors. These snippets included some of Michelangelo's own poetry in a new English translation – 'My beard extends heavenward; my nape falls in/fixed on my spine, and visibly my sternum/ becomes like a harp ... [Insert FX: *twanging*]' run the lines according to my production notes. All of these tracks would be played via discreet headsets that visitors wear and fiddle with at their leisure as they wander past the artworks.

I am neither an actor nor an art historian. I checked the paperwork of both my brief and my contract three times and it's clear that my name will not be appearing in the credits of these audio guides. Fair enough. Foley artists are employed as a surreptitious service and our anonymity seems fitting, somehow – I only ever get work precisely because I blend in unobtrusively. If you ever hear the sound of rain on the radio or see rain during a film, chances are that a Foley artist has spent some time sprinkling rice or sand on a cooking tray so that you get to experience the *rainiest* rain that ever rained without the sound dominating the scene. Those cosy TV Christmas specials or period dramas with their crackling fireplaces? That sound will have been added in post-production and what you are actually hearing is me crouched over a sensitive microphone and scrunching wads of baking parchment. When a character walks through snow on screen, imagine me by a microphone stamping up and down on a thick layer of cat litter. When that character slips and breaks their leg, the sound that causes you to wince was made by me snapping a piece of celery in a wet tea towel.

The final recordings that the gallery will use are recorded in the studio, a small room filled to the brim with baffle, but I do like to trial various first drafts and experiments for specific sounds at home. For this Michelangelo commission I had great fun yesterday trying to convey the sound of metal ladders being pulled up from the damned as pictured in *The Last Judgment* and that of angels' long-stemmed trumpets knocking the heads of the elect. I found the right sound for this latter action by bouncing the bowl of a ladle against the top of my IKEA wine rack. The quiet, heavy swish of fabric that accompanies an art historian's discussion of Michelangelo's *Pietà* statue will be made by flexing my mother's Laura Ashley curtains between my hands.

There was one more Foley track that I had not recorded. It was one that had not been requested – the production notes for the *Creation of Eve* image state I should select some 'Mediterranean/English garden birdsong (morning) FX' and the sound of a river from stock audio files. I compared these notes for the *Creation of Eve* to those compiled for the *Creation of Adam* painting. Visitors who hit the button when looking at the more famous painting would literally receive all the bells and whistles. Loud gongs, clashing cymbals! Timpani and choirs! All that plus a Teslacoil crackle would be stuffed through the wires in the visitor's earphones to signify Adam and God networking on a cloud and showing each other their nipples, going in for the first corporate handshake.

The imbalance of attention lavished between the two *Creations* struck me as unfair. I have a hazy memory of the myth about the birth of Eve, that of a lonely man clutching his side in a garden and asking that a helpmate be Deliverood unto him. As I ordered a takeaway last night and considered for a millisecond whether I could put the cost on research expenses, I looked up the relevant Bible verse to check what was said as per Eve springing into being. And how has Michelangelo chosen to show it? Perhaps God whittled her from Adam's rib, or perhaps He passed the rib back to the freshly filleted Adam to be whittled. As a test I experimented sliding a pair of chopsticks across one another next to the microphone but the sound was too much like knitting to seem fitting for the miracle of rib-becomes-woman. Maybe God and Adam, wearing nothing but gardening gloves and with all the time in the new world for navel-gazing, planted the rib in the Eden soil and she took root right there and grew up like a shoot. Or the rib might have rolled out of Adam's side and Mandelbrot-fractalled into something bigger, its small curve of bone flinging out sudden rib-promontories and dendrites the very moment that it hit the earth until it achieved the shape of a fully formed woman.

What were the presumed mechanics, and how might an understanding of them help me decide on a Foley track? What is the Foley equivalent of a posed rhetorical question?

I dog-eared the printout of the *Creation of Eve* and listened to that action's sound, the minute noise of paper yielding to itself. I rapped my day-old, tooth-stripped #34 Char Siu takeaway rib against the microphone and watched the levels on my computer screen jump with surprise. Michelangelo's Eve looks a bit like me, I thought. I wondered about the model the artist might have used in his sketches to capture her posture. Distractedly I gnawed on the meatless rib in my hand. She looks like someone who might chew her nails and stub her toes, like she too mistakenly shampoos her hair twice instead of using conditioner because sometimes she neglects to check which bottle she is using. She is painted, presumably, taking a first momentous gasp of Mediterranean/English garden breath but her expression is not momentous. It is small and aghast. It is the expression of someone slightly worried that they might have given the cat fleas rather than the other way around. I turned the printout over and looked at the blank back of the page, and read my word *BAFFLE* underlined twice. It was a cheap printout. You could see a faint trace of Eve's outline through the paper.

In the image Eve is painted standing at Adam's side with her arms raised, palms together as if caught in a dance move or as if shot out of a very slow, lumbersome rib-cannon. It is the posture of one who is diving, or perhaps slightly hunched in supplication. She is playing Charades, gamely, against her will, and her audience is having none of it. I compare my own posture at my desk, takeaway rib between my teeth and slumped over my microphone. God is painted facing Eve and it looks like He is giving her a noncommittal ticking-off. He gets to wear clothes but has bare feet. Presumably Eden is turfed with comfy lawns. Adam lies lolling in a tousled, sidekick slumber to the left of the picture. He does not show any obvious signs of surgery or happy fatherhood. Unlike Eve and God he appears expressionless, merely tired after a day of naming things whatever the hell he likes.

I flipped the printout over because the whiteness of its underside was scaring me. I read in my research notes that Michelangelo once made a snowman. He sculpted it in a Florence courtyard for one of the Medici. Blank-faced and temporary, it must have melted into priceless gutters. I brought the printout up to my eye and saw that the paintwork was covered in spider-leg fractures. I thought about the crack in my bedroom ceiling and about five hundred years of worshippers looking up God's skirts and togas, pointing out and naming their favourite saints.

I felt a growing unnamed impatience that the allotted sounds I had been tasked to provide for this landscape – the vague birdsong and river splashings – did not seem enough of a tribute to the scene. Not to this Eve, disribbed for his pleasure and of whom I had become fond, nor for the sounds of unseen birth and the concept of a floating rib, the body's hitchhikers. I wanted the visitors in the gallery to draw closer to this image when they listened to the suggested soundscape, not skip this track or use it as filler for dawdle time as they moved on to the more famous *Creation*'s boom and pomp or the to-scale version of *David*'s contrapposto mooch. There is the suggestion of a river's tributary or some blue remembered hills beyond the figures. Their tableau takes place beneath the calm-before-storm clouds of a sin-scrumping morning. I wanted to find a sound that would stand tribute to soft paintbrushes on newborn skin and to reluctant rib-ticklers everywhere. The more I looked at Eve's expression, the more she seemed to be saying to her maker *Please put me back*. Or *what have you done*?

'Lament,' said the tree branch a third time at my window. 'One two, one two,' I said to check the levels. I looked a final time at the picture of the naked couple and their clothed onlooker. I thought about the cracked plaster of my bedroom ceiling, and the lack of my name in the production credits, and I did not feel ashamed.

Ensuring that the microphone was at the correct angle, I put my finger in my cheek, flicked my wrist and I recorded a short, absurd *pop*.

Smote

(or When I Find I Cannot Kiss You In Front Of A Print By Bridget Riley)

To kiss you should not involve such fear of imprecision. I shouldn't mind about the gallery attendant. He is not staring. That's not the reason that he carries a torch and lanyard on his belt.

I have seen at least four people holding hands already and I'm only just out of the revolving doors. Were they revolving, or sliding? I have a memory of having to shoulder as I stepped forward. The four people holding hands weren't unpeeling to the root. To kiss you should not feel like anything other than embellishment. They – people, loads of people – have staged kiss-ins at Sainsbury's and in Southbank cafes precisely in solidarity with my freedom to kiss you. They even kissed en masse on Valentine's Day with a hashtag and everything. When that historian shot himself in Notre Dame two years ago, when Larousse dictionary mooted changing the definition of marriage, he was not thinking about me tarrying in this gallery's gift shop, flicking postcards and studiously not-looking at you.

Larousse dictionary's colophon is a woman blowing at a dandelion clock. Have I used the word *colophon* correctly? Where are you?

Dandelion comes from the French *dent-de-lion*, lion's tooth.

I am not biding my time.

A lion would not baulk at kissing you, toothily. The French for dandelion is *pissenlit*. This translates, broadly, as *wet the bed*. I will wait.

I could kiss you lightly, the side of your face, as if putting out a fire. The gallery attendant is not looking at us. I have spotted another couple not only holding hands but kissing, a boy and a girl, like it was nothing, like they didn't have to think about lions.

When you puff at a dandelion clock, puff at its puff, it looks like you are blowing a kiss. To kiss you would be plotlessness, and nothing like falling. The gallery attendant is not sizing up our haircuts. In fact, he's looking the other way.

The move was mine to make,

all gallery-hushed and happy as I reached for you and

RIGHT

LET'S but

out of the corner of my cordoned-off sight, my

– all my resolution –

is suddenly just right angles – an eyeline a little botched – what *is* all this – this jaw swerve chicanery and all at once it's sugar cubes and squares of basalt in a line, monochrome shapes aligned as teeth in a first taste of treacle toffee, a sucker punch that crazy-paves the direct route that means I stand here having steeled myself when I would will every word be cursive and supple and tender but now all my letters are strung out with rigid symmetry, bending, tined as the strongest parts of my spine finding the spin of optic tic-shout unframing itself beyond your ear, behind your ear, [THIS IS ALREADY RATHER EMBARRASSING BECAUSE] how could you frame such a thing, I mean a painting, or a print, that has thumbed such a serried bank of vacuums into the wall just by being nailed there, there, where I can see something in this painting rolling along the wall as though the muscles in the chew of a maw (that is *maw* M-A-W not A-M-O-R-E, if you were asking, but you're not, you're looking, not at me nor at the lion-couple you are just clear-eyed and looking at a beyondness) made of lines on a wall – I did not know hand could hold hand but also *not*-hold like this, standing in a gallery, when looking at a painting so regular and simple, not-looking directly at you and not directly thinking how, *how*, then, when I move to take your unbold shoulder and the attendant is quite so *attendant* and the painting is quite so unwatchable I cannot stand to be here looking there standing in front of a painting the surface of which itches with vertigo, seeing suddenly that there is a weft to its spirit-level: looking at this painting over your shoulder and taking your hand is like trying to taste wordplay or suffering snow-blindness with your hands, it's like the Northern Line on the Tube map unfurling and crosshatching the city and as I steady my eye-line I fall for you through straight lines to something hillocked and tussocked and wispy and girdled and girderful and dog-eared because it's all there in black and white, houndstooth fabric spoked with clock hands smoothing and then rumpled as over your shoulder the *Movement in Squares* (1961) by Bridget Riley becomes a vinyl record's surface gleaming white as if the light was bouncing from it but in fact, now, I think it has become a broken disc or spiders' legs across fresh bed linen, a capital letter first person I becoming a forward slash, an exclamation mark becoming a backstroke because I find I cannot kiss you standing by this painting, I would start bleeding salt and pepper although I could imagine kissing you by other gentler, less queer checker-boards, by hazy Hammershøi's windowpanes, by Sarah Lucas's *Self Portrait with Fried Eggs* (1996), by Vermeer's *The Allegory of Painting* (c. 1665–1668) and in the marble checkerboard-spelt-with-a-*k* or chequerboard-spelt-with-a-*q* hallways always queuing-up the next opportunity rather than being quite up for it there, *in situ*, mindlessly, I have gone too far to pull back, I could kiss you under severe black and white patchwork quilts so why not *here*, with you wearing black and white gingham and me wearing Walt Jabsco ska-suspenders, working out skunk-back Rubik's Cubes on a headboard, but! I, despite myself, I find I am now all mouthfuls of sinister made-for-purpose ludicrous black and white-checked Battenberg cake, I am squaring up, I am *not* holding you but holding onto you for fear of slip-ping, parallelographic graphite zest, Stendhal Syndroming at the thought of you by this painting and my lips anywhere near yours, the gallery attendant and his lion eyes and the painting sewing up my heart with false orthogonals, darts, black runnels in snow made for a moleskin-night-time when to hold you here is a game of chess on a grumbling crum-bling glacier, the gambit's gone your way and I am bishop-fumbled rook-to-h8, stalemate giddy, I might as well be pushing marzipan through an iron portcullis, I might as well be kissing you through a trellis, I might as well be pushing you up against a snaggle-toothed grinning and ruined keyboard with apologies for any cross-posting, with all just potholed covers of Abbey Road album crossings and we cannot arrange the pulp of black and white things like dragon fruit nor custard apples nor humbugs on a plate, 'not in a *gallery*, think of the children!', and it is Guinness-thick the choke of it, it is as strange as your hand in mine, all pirated copies of *The Seventh Seal* that twist and bulge with white noise interface and interference, the squeak of it: something like dandelion seeds on velvet, like lions' breath steaming in the night, like vanilla pods and icing sugar, something like black rye bread grout-thick with white butter, something like black kelp crawling up against the humped sea foam on a white tide, a nocturne's stave in a key made mazy and thick with dieses, a printout made tweedy with hashtags, my hand, clumsy with a melting tessellation, I think, *goddammit Bridget Riley* (1961), my hand with a melting tessellation could feed you crushed Oreos and moon parings, my hand not quite in yours, but not yet quite out, the starting flag at the race track when a white flag means surrender and Black Flag means punk bands formed in seventies' California and I cannot tell whether you or I are leaning now nor if the attendant is approaching or I just think he is, or if I am staggering into the falling and unfair taut roiling of a painting, its good lines like tarmac heating through a drift of snow or a sky thick and slick with black and white *Pontia protodice* butterflies, piebald horses on an oil slick, and in this second's thought I could have – rather than grown anxious and aware of the attendant – dreamt of dressing you in coats trimmed with lemur tails and em dashes, corner you in fields filled and frilled with Friesian cows and badgers' scalps and California king snakes, and this is absurd, this is all absurd and that's the power of it, the checking of my hand in your hand because I'm sure there are rules about this kind of thing on a noticeboard somewhere, that we can ignore, and others can misread and it'll all be there in black and white, the empty page so daunting, the full page so disappointing, a new moon seen through eyelashes or many moons grated by one eyelash welted and unbelted and wrought through space's hot static of white noise's rough and tumble tumbril wheelings, the white and black of it bletting the Whitsun eiderdown even as I watch it, the pairing of us before this painting, behind your shoulder, through your hair, striations, despite the gallery attendant leaning in – I cannot find the angle of your jaw in a way that isn't calming: I do not want to calm any part of you in this gallery when this painting could autocorrect the clouds outside the Tate into order, make us greyscale and plaid-eyed and with ears full of Sillitoe Tartan's klaxon blare or all new ceramic and sable-fur, like eggshells on the kerbside, like charcoal in the cream, like bone in the coffee where headlong, and garbled, on the gallery wall, geometry curdles and all that I am, you have made italic. Holding you here is to make a chequered past. I will never be brave and I cannot kiss you by this painting.

You have leaned in, and have kissed me without even thinking about it like it is the easiest thing in the world

and you stark me
and I am strobe-hearted

and as you move on to the next painting and the gallery attendant fiddles with his watch, a Bridget Riley grows a little cooler on the wall and all in all you spectrum me, unexpectedly.

Bs

I was awake for three reasons.

One: you live near a Tube stop and it was firing up for the first journey of the day. Two: there's a bird in the tree outside your window and it was shouting at your house. I don't know what kind of bird it was, nor the type of tree. Thirdly: you had trapped a bee in a glass last night and forgotten to let it out. The intention was clearly there, to transport it down the stairs or tip it out of the window, and you had slid a postcard of Vienna or St. Petersburg or that sort of place beneath the tumbler in readiness. It was not actually a tumbler at all but a washed-out jar of Nutella and the bee was drunk on a whole night's worth of staring at the sights of Vienna or St. Petersburg and the city's ghosts of hazelnuts and sugar, *dink-d'dink-dinking* its head against a transparent wall on your bedside table. Trapped beneath your arm, I blinked at the bee. Bees can see in UV light so we must have looked like a ridiculous disco last night. It headbanged an answer to this thought, eyes all honeycombed and asterisk-star-kaleidoscopic while outside the bird shouted a little louder.

I'm sure there is an identification app that allows you to run through an index of birds' toccatas and scherzos and bugled blurts. As you thumb down the list, little facts about birds might run in a scrolling marquee along the bottom of your screen. *The bones of a pigeon weigh less than its feathers*, that kind of thing. Starlings only exist in America because a man wanted to introduce all the birds mentioned in Shakespeare's plays to the continent. The organ in a bird's throat that allows it to sing is a called a *syrinx* – I test this word now between my teeth and feel it is far sprightlier and more lovely a word than *larynx*. This was a good call on the anatomists' part. You stir as I say *larynx* aloud and turn a little, causing crowfeet folds in your pillow around your head. Sleepily, I wonder whether there could be an equivalent app for identifying bees by their song before remembering that they do not sing. Not for us, anyway. They dance. I make a note to look up bee facts later in the day for balance's sake.

Just yesterday I read a study that found older honeybees effectively reverse brain-aging when they take on those nest responsibilities that are typically handled by much younger bees. *Beebrain*, I say softly out loud, and the crowfeet of your pillow deepen imperceptibly.

I always thought that birdsong was supposed to be lovely but here was this blackbird-slash-thrush-slash-starling-slash-finch going full alarm-alarum crazy. I can't believe you stirred at *larynx* and *beebrain* but can sleep right through this going on outside your window.

Maybe the unseen bird had carved BIRD 4 BEE 4EVA with its beak on the tree trunk outside in a big old notch-heart. Or perhaps it was shouting the passerine equivalent of *OI, MATE, ARE YOU LOOKING AT MY BEE?* and the bee is performing a mournful balloné and brisé on a Venetian or Peterburgian balcony while I'm tangled up here caught in the euphemisms and innuendos of the shadows of a pillow, only half-awake and thinking that I should leave. The bird and the bee could set up, I think, a lovely B&B and serve their guests toast with honey and eggs.

Who am I to keep them apart? I thought.

A bee in the hand worth two in the bonnet, I think, and I pick up the glass and stumble to the window that is not mine and NOW! the window is OPEN! and the glass is OVERTURNED! and the bee has flown out by my ear and become a comma in the air, and the blackbird-slash-thrush-slash-starling-slash-finch joined it in the air, and the commuters at the station beneath your window applauded the bee and the bird and the considerate naked woman with her arms flung out framed in the window above their platform, as if this was an opera, and then the same commuters stepped into their train and the curved glass of the carriage doors shut behind them, and all of this is a half-asleep thought of a euphemism of a metaphor of a ghost of the word for the sight of you opening an eye and saying 'Good morning', and that the thought of you as a bird, or as a bee, might always be worth waking to.

Alight at the Next

When the carriage doors do their thing, it being after hours
when my thinking is unsavoury and also far from sweet,
knowing we are at the stop nearest my house and I'm going
to have to summon the courage to ask you to come back, the
whole cadence of my composed speech set to work in time
with the slowing of the Tube train, the slowing with a
whinge of –

not-hinges but a kind of mechanical sighing and when
the doors

Please mind –

when the doors are opening and you are standing closer to
me than you ever have, and I have been counting, and meas-
uring, and the doors have opened and

// a man // pushes on // to get inside // the carriage
before I've had time // to step down

so without thinking and certainly without hinges I am holding out my hand and placing a finger in the middle of his forehead.

He freezes. The carriage freezes; a carriage steamed-up and bulbous with umbrellas and the slapping batskin wings of waterproof jackets.

The man doesn't look in my eyes, because this is London, dammit, but he halts, there, one shoe up in the train –

I look like I'm blessing him.
I hope no one thinks I'm blessing him.
I hope you don't think I do this regularly, you
standing so irregularly close to me like this –

The angle of the man's nose is precisely forty-five degrees. This was distracting; I wish someone had a protractor so I could show you how precisely at forty-five degrees this man's nose was but who carries protractors on the District Line? And what kind of pervert even knew what the set square in the school geometry set was for unless one is the daughter of a naval architect or wanting to prove the angle of a man's nose inches, Imperial inches, from one's own –

I wish not for the first time that London had bars or, at a push, a wooden buffet carriage on the Tube because I would keep my finger there against his forehead, hold out my other hand and perhaps you might slide a whisky down across the bar to me and I would drink it and I would pull my hat down as your arm came across my shoulder to show you that we were a crack team at getting the Tube to my stop, that we were as good as Bonnie and Clyding this evening –

(this thought breaks down when I remember I don't like whiskey, spelled with an *e* or without)

(this Bonnie and Clyde metaphor breaks down too when I remember that the real-life Clyde, in jail, in order to get out of breaking rocks, took a spade and cut off some of his own toes)

(I would not want you to have a toeless lover)

(I want you to have a lover who can *stop* this man in his suit and tie)

(I want you to have a lover who is not embarrassed to say the word *lover* in a carriage filled with tired, final-round West Londoners)

and this man

this *awful* man in a tie that's red

and if I squint down at it <<<
the tie {{{{
past his set-square 45° nose >>>
the tie looks like a botched tracheotomy
dribbling past his –

No – that's not fair, it's a nice tie and he just has somewhere, someone to get to and I just want to seem like a person that can stand up for themselves on the Tube let alone keep standing when you are really, *you really are standing so close to me* –

It used to have 'Mind The Gap' written at this station in yellow on the platform edge but now it says 'Mind the step'. The difference is crucial: even the platform is a coward and uses polite, shirking rhetoric and less capitalisation now even as my finger is still on his forehead and the doors are shutting, and I will miss my –

we'll both miss *my stop*

and I might lose a finger, but Clyde of 'Bonnie and' fame lost some toes and I might be played by Warren Beatty some day so I give this man's forehead a little jab, the smallest pressure

(he has not met my eyes this whole time like someone
has thrown the book at him before)

and I make a boiled sound because I am the first to admit that my spirit animal is probably a buttered roll and that I create characters and situations where I am brave for the same reasons some people love the stuffing of caught birds. Pigeons get caught on the carriages sometimes: I've seen it with my Oyster in my pocket, spring in my steptoes. I forget sometimes what *preclude* and *nascent* mean. It has been a long day for everybody, even for pigeons, and it is forgetfulness that makes me brave at the sound of this gamelan of joists and hot-steamed-grit-zoom that is pulling into stations. I am certainly braver than before, when the pre-you afternoon got jumbled with you-evening at rush hour, where throats squirmed with the old smoke and stream of tunnels: a world pinstriped by eyelashes, uproarious with the need for a Friday, downroarius with lost cards –

there are earphones trailing from this man's neck and
they squeak with chords that have the obtuse delicacy
of a dove retching –

the thought of you unscrews my head

> and if you record the rip of glacier through ice and
> modulate its frequency it sounds of whale-song, and
> we often have cause to think of glaciers and their
> place and pace on the District Line –

We are still here with my ET finger set against his forehead. He does not wear a wedding ring and I construct a reality for him wherein he, after an argument with his wife, stamped out of the house and tried to remove the ring, could not, had to buy a cheap bottle of salad cream at the cornershop by his Tube station to use as lubricant so that he might loosen it from his hand.

I had one drink this evening so it's unlikely to be the stout that makes me brave or foolhardy, stout that tasted feminine, of ashtrays, bran and old lipstick. You are so clever, I remember thinking, badly. You are so clever and you know so much, and I often think the only way that I could protect you (if you ever asked [because, you know, you would never need to be protected, and would kick me for trying – you are certainly standing close enough]) would be to snap your head off and roll it out of harm's way for the nation's sake.

I forgot. I simply forgot the way that love becomes a whimsy and the full-throttle of throats, the buzz of flightless eyelashes against pillowcases on a winter's evening when pigeons grow full-fat against the frost and the letter *p* in the word *receipt* begins ticking at the clocked teeth, the watched rim of a clock when I wake up to find the time, from being a cameo in my own dreams where I occasionally look straight to camera and spoil the shot. I forgot about waking to dumb punk dawns – me, a hopeless sometimes-son-type whose act is hardly ever there delivering UNHEIMLICH MANOEUVRES like this finger on the centre of this man's forehead.

Somewhere beyond us an escalator squeals, a pushchair squeals, the child in the pushchair squeals. I only did not squeal because you really are standing so very close.

Look how far my arms can go around things, I want to say. I could hug a whole telephone box. I have had too much, perhaps, of the good stuff and Lord knows there's a lot of the world we're missing as I do something important with this here man in this here tunnel:

for example, we're missing an overly busy sky, with a warp and a weft to it. Like tweed. Starlings making a tweed of the sky.

For example, we're missing a snail insisting that he's in the haulage business

we're missing drinking hot chocolate in the continental way, kissing in a gorse bush

we're missing chewing gum until my jaw is black and
blue and the world is tired mint, District Line-
coloured, but

THROWAWAY LINES like this WILL BE ALL
RIGHT

because

today, my eyes are chintz; today, my eyes are
tigerskin; today, my eyes are traitors; today my eyes
are Delftware and he's met them, finally

(is *beneathe* a verb?

perhaps I'm thinking of *bequeath* or *breathe*).

Each of his eyelashes is a candlewick and now I find that I cannot look at him full-on in case I press my heart out through my teeth.

And time passes, in and out of consciousness and the
man steps back, and the Tube doors doors shut

and you really were standing so very close to me as
the train moved, itself, beneatheing.

Concision

One single Finnish word describes the sudden blast of heat that comes after water is poured upon a sauna's brazier. One Bantu verb can be used to sum up the act of discarding one's clothes specifically in order to dance, while on Easter Island one Rapa Nui word means 'the swelling of the larynx caused by screaming too much'.

I am anchored to my spot by the landline and we both know that there's nothing that I can say to save the conversation from its course, so instead I pass the time putting my eye to the three holes in the telephone receiver. You are speaking and I am staring, the wire coiled through my fingers connecting our present tenses. You are using short sentences and I blink in time with each clause – I blink directly against the plastic of the phone so that you might hear the kissing scrape of eyelashes. I am quick to replace my eye with my mouth to calm you when I detect the wheedle of your voice becomes pitched more urgently.

I look at the hand that is holding the phone with a new curiosity. It is holding the curved plastic to my face with a grip that I would usually only ever associate with times of panic. I know, through some previous spurious training, that should I ever find myself wandering on to quicksand, I must endeavour to lie flat, not struggle and try to gain purchase on a nearby bough or rope. Such is my grip on the telephone receiver now – the receiver is an overhanging branch just as it is a branch sprung from the stronger trunk of my wrist. It is also something blooming twin-budded with my mouth and ear at either end. Both buds are flapping, receiving and transmitting. Venus flytraps; my mouth and my ear.

I wait for you to speak once more and for our conversation to present itself through tenses of our throats and flicks at the three delicate bones of the inner ear – we attend the clicks of underwater cables and teeth and caveats and I sit there eyeing the telephone in my hand and waiting for your final line.

You are waiting for mine.

The body of the telephone is black and squat and it is shiny. I didn't like liquorice as a child and always spat it into my hand. I confided this fact to you when we first met, and you told me that you did exactly the same with Mint Imperials. The table on which my spat-liquorice shiny telephone sits has been in this position by the window for so long that its legs have notched crop circles into the carpet. I tried to work out the total number of hours I must have sat in this precise position over the years. I must have perched on the arm of this sofa by the phone like this for weeks, making sure not to struggle or draw lines in the sand.

There is a change in sound and I find that you have hung up, and I am poised to not-speak to the absence of you with the cord of the phone still hanging heavy in my hand.

I put my eye to the holes punched into the receiver and square my shoulders, attempting to stare down the dialling tone. The holes in the phone look like a series of black moons or umlauts trailing in the wake of your absent vowels, or maybe Alice's rabbit hole, or the magician's hat from which one might pull a rabbit. A nostril in plastic, a pore, a piercing, the round cross-hair in opening credits.

My body is shocked that you hung up. My mouth is caught open, mid-howl or mid-coo or attempting a parody of the hole in the receiver.

By now I can hear the subtleties within this dialling tone in the same way that I can recognise the intonations of your laugh or the curve of your fingerprint or of your spine. It is the well-read blurb of you. The dialling tone makes a tuning fork of my head.

In isolation, one of the holes in the phone's plastic looks like a full stop. An exclamation mark is a full stop with a cockatoo's crest. Full stops, three full-stops. Had you been waiting for me to finish your sentence and to join the dots?

Lichtenstein or Seurat or the sign of a *therefore*'s stacked notation, used to indicate the conclusion of a syllogism. You can't see the whole picture without counting on the importance of dots, motes, specks.

Sitting by the phone, I must have steeled myself because I did not lie flat on my front or on my back but drew my knees beneath my chin and tried to mote myself, sucking in my stomach. Black holes in space, I think, are right now sucking on something and everyone is in awe of *them*. The pupil is an absence in your eye. I wonder if I will see that dot again, or tell you that I know every flex of its absence. It's the 'That's All, Folks!' black hole into which a cartoon pig giggles, stutters, disappears. These dots in this lickerish plastic are suddenly your laugh, the dangling bell-rope of your throat, or it's a river-smoothed disc of black stone that would skip like a heartbeat if skimmed across a flat enough surface. The places that your business trips have taken you! Places with Venus flytraps and sinking stinking sand – I used to have an Atlas under the phone just so I could trace the contour lines and tributaries around your location as you spoke to me, and as I nodded along with your words I would work out our time differences with the small, flat pocket calculator branded with your company's name which you pocketed at a conference and I used as a bookmark. Over the years, you had called me from street corners and from busy cafes and from echoing conference venues.

I wondered whether you had made this particular call in a place that was near water with skippable stones or somewhere that might serve you the black circle of an espresso on a white table.

I put my eye again to the receiver and pretended it could be a periscope and that I could have seen the moment that your hand slammed down the receiver at your end. This is perhaps a mischaracterisation – maybe you simply eased it, gently, back in its moorings. The sense of depth that these holes have is not quite filled with your side of the story. I hope you were not gentle with the phone at your end. I hope my silence made you angry, and that these holes in the plastic are the phone's 'Ooo!' of camp surprise that you dared to smash the phone down with such violence.

On the road outside my house, the traffic lights stack their circles like the beads of a necklace and the sun does something pale and total behind a cloud. I clicked my jaw and closed my mouth. In short – you waited for me to return the goodbye and when you realised I couldn't, you hung up.

One single Finnish word describes the sudden blast of heat that comes after water is poured upon a sauna's brazier. One Bantu verb can be used to sum up the act of discarding one's clothes specifically in order to dance, while on Easter Island there is a Rapa Nui word that means 'the swelling of the larynx caused by screaming too much'.

So: *löyly, mbuki-mvuki, ngaobera*. I think I hear each of these words in the 90Hz of the dialling tone as I lift the lack of your voice from my face, take breath and return the receiver to its cradle.

And Back Again

Now: thoughts of a porch, the back-damp luggage that I might have brought and a different flavour of sunlight on my skin as I wait for the hotel to open.

Then: you had asked an easy question about love and a song lyric had entered my head.

'This much,' had been my initial response and I extended my arms as far as they would go, which could never be enough but let the record show it was roughly five foot seven inches and you had not looked impressed. I was embarrassed that I had attempted measurement and turned my head back to my laptop screen. Of course there could be no quantifying it – you were looking for rhetoric not wingspans – there are only things you can do for it or give up for it, not units – deeds, quests, behests, not *measurements*. That is the moment when the song had slipped into my head and I knew what I had to do. Reaching for you gingerly as I am no good at hugs, holding out a hand to your shoulders as if you were a house of cards or something snappable beneath water, I told you that I thought I could prove my quality if not love's quantity in a way the world would recognise.

And so to thoughts of a strange porch in the West African sunshine.

I had every hope that my idea was original. No doubt I would arrive to find my hotel in Timbuktu with a room already made-up specifically for people arriving on missions identical to my own. Each of us would think that we're being highly novel in our undertaking, West End musicals influencing the West African tourist industry one chorus lyric at a time, but the hotel would get about three of us a month, all looking equally lovelorn and with similar cheap straw hats. I might even find a commemorative poster of the original 1960 *Oliver!* West End cast tacked to the wardrobe door in the room I was led to. The receptionist would look up from his crossword with complete disinterest when I asked whether he could take a photo of me with a map of the city to send on to you as evidence that I was here.

I would pose with two thumbs up.

The last *Oliver!* pilgrim might have left a battered copy of Camus behind on the bedspread. The book could look untouched: spotless, a prop. I'm clumsy so within a week would have broken its spine and dropped it in the bath. The hotel might provided a cassette with the song on it.

I'll do anything,
For you, dear, anything

On my first evening in this fictional hotel I would eat the foamy shrimp Pick'n'Mix that I'd bought at the airport and watch the street beneath my window. The evening sky, I imagine, might grow purple at the edges and before long rain would begin hitting the windowsill. I might watch huge raindrops make coronets in the dirt before it smoothed the whole road below into bright red water.

Timbuktu, cockatoo, tickety-boo. The city's name is a word that charms and comes bubbly and saffron-scented against the tongue. I know so little of the place beyond its name, and yet I can fantasise every detail of the cheap hotel room I might find there. In this hotel room, I would sing the all-important line to myself and go to bed.

I know that I'll go anywhere,
For your smile, anywhere,
For your smile's everywhere I see.

After a week in the hotel room, I have a notion that insects would have eaten a hole in my straw hat and pressed their little librarian-stamp deposits on the copy of Camus, by which I mean, with no poetic extension, that the insects would have shat in my predecessor's book. When I switch on the light at midnight, I might hear them scuttling away from me then *plinkety-plinkety shh* as they scoot down the sink plughole. *You* would know how to calm me down but given I would have travelled here alone I would not be able to sleep knowing that they're there. The overhead fan might slice the air into swallowable rashers and this world I'm imagining would be divided into a million squares through the grille of my mosquito net.

Timbucktootle: the sound of the craze-plumed starlings outside. I suppose that I would be at my window a lot of the time during my stay and the starlings would regard me with cocked heads. I imagine starlings are the same everywhere (you are not here to correct me). Did you know Timbuktu is twinned with Hay-on-Wye? Such a sky I swear I could fly, me oh my. I wonder if you remember that day we once visited the book festival there, uninsected paperbacks in our pockets. We had watched a flock of starlings make strange shapes and polygons and digressions against an evening's clouds. Maybe I'm basing my ideas of a hotel room in Mali on my memories of a B&B in Wales. My horizons are so small and stuffy. *Who can say where she may hide? Must I travel far and wide? 'Til I am beside the someone who I can mean something to?*

But in this daydream, say, where I know things beyond my philosophies, each day that I stay in my fictional Timbuktu hotel I might see a truck advertising *La Vache*

Qui Rit cheese draw up at first light. Let's say the driver would jump out wearing a turquoise T shirt. He might look at the picture of *La Vache* on the truck and give her a familiar pat on the ear. I might spot him that evening in the hotel bar and he would tell me that his shirt is a Chelsea away strip, specifying the years 2005–2006 very gravely. He could ask whether I'm from England, then whether I've ever been to Stamford Bridge. He might look disappointed by my second answer and ask me why I've travelled here. He could laugh for five minutes straight when I tell him the reason but add that he approves of my plan to paint my face bright blue. We could have another drink as I tell him about things to do in Hay-on-Wye and he would patiently smoke clove-scented cigarettes, and when the last of our bottles' froth has been flicked from the table he could offer me a lift into the city in his truck. I could leave the hotel. I could imagine more. I could do some actual research. He could watch as I hesitate on my concept of a Timbuktu hotel's porch, considering my options.

Let's say a corsair moon would be doing scimitar practice above us and the stars would be like anvil sparks. It could have been market day during daylight hours and I'd watched it all going on below my room. There could have been fourteen hundred different coloured fabrics, and the voices of the city could have risen to my window in haggles with accompanying shrugs and outspread, counting fingers.

Within this extended metaphor I could shout down to one trader to ask whether they had any bottle-openers as I would have broken the one supplied for the mini-bar – he might throw up a penknife to me and I would aim my cash at his head. The knife might, say, have a picture of a vulture on it, and I would use it to beckon my new *Vache Qui Rit* friend back indoors to open another final beer for him. Market day might mean that the whole hotel lobby that I have daydreamed would smell of roasted goat and the atomised clay of the road.

Would you climb a hill?
Anything!
Wear a daffodil?
Anything!
Leave me all your will?
Anything!
Even fight my Bill?
What? Fisticuffs?
I'd risk everything for one kiss; everything;
Yes, I'd do anything –

The last time that I had seen you, as I had said goodbye I knelt down and tied your shoe. You had made me straighten. You said, not laughingly, that I didn't have to prove anything let alone in a way that was based on lines from a musical.

When I said that I disagreed you had – quite correctly – pointed out that tying a shoe as I had just done didn't really count because I had also *untied* it first to make the action possible and also that the shoes in question were fastened with Velcro. This was an unideal beginning but by then I'd made my mind up. I had decided on my metaphor.

Would you lace my shoe?
Anything!
Paint your face bright blue?
Anything!
Catch a kangaroo?
Anything!
Go to Timbuktu?

Over our beers, the Timbuktu Chelsea fan might tell me I was crazy and say that you wouldn't care if I didn't follow my plan to show my mettle. *How will you catch a kangaroo anyway?*, he might ask, and laugh again. He would have a point. He might say that he could take me out to see the city, that I could go to the actual city, and that he would act as my guide. I could swim in a bottomless pool, fringed by pearl-white rocks. There was a saint's relic housed in a silver book not five minutes from the hotel door, he might say, and a museum that held an emerald as thick as a horse's neck. He would know a cafe where they made a drink so fizzy it would make you hiccup for a week and in the basement – if you knew the right secret knock – there were men in suits betting money on gecko races. He might say that he could show me how to tell a mirage from an oasis and that I could toss a coin down a local well that was haunted by a shaman's strangled daughter. I could grow up, stop fantasising, do my research properly and realise that Mali was a warzone.

The receptionist at my imagined Timbuktu hotel might shout over to our table that the *Oliver!* pilgrims were never interested in seeing the city. I would look at my feet and my new friend might despair.

The coffee in Timbuktu might be sweet and black and poured into tiny glasses. At night I would have to wrestle mosquitoes the size of bulldogs. They would fry audibly on the street-lamps outside. I would probably break any cassette by playing it too much.

Let's say I would be at the window and thinking about the Chelsea shirt, the foamy shrimp, Brecknockshire starlings and *La Vache Qui Rit*. They help ground me, which is good, because the idea of the real city beyond them invites flighty hyperbole, paroxysms of exoticism and something unpolluted which is not what I wanted from my trip. I hope I would have scoured the hotel for distractions – there might be an English dictionary, a (how convenient) copy of *The Birds of Africa* and a French Bible in the lobby to add to the Camus. The bird book might say that vultures are scavengers, churlish and bald with pulled-down mouths, but also that they will not eat the dead of their own species. There is a certain nobility in recognising one's own flesh as tasteless. This might be Camus rubbing off on me, however. The word *Timbuktu* comes just before *time* in the dictionary. Back home when I was fictionally booking the fictional tickets for this fictional flight, I would have thought that the word *TIMBUKTU* had the rhythm of a squirrel-hop or a newly boiled kettle clicking itself off. Mundane sounds. It has just the right mix of spiked and undulating letters to imply travel, however. Flight of fancy in its shape – *TIMBUKTU*, the verticals of boat masts riding easy waves, railway tracks lying between banking hillsides.

If you were here perhaps I'd be able to leave my idea of the hotel. I would dream about you visiting on my last night, and of us hitting the town, outlandishly. Neither of us would sunburn and our hair and clothes would stay dry and smell of tamarind. I'd

hy –
perbole
for you,
here

in the desert where we might gather ostrich feathers, roll down dunes, feel the sun through our eyelids and kick sand into the stars – we'd weave mosquito nets from camels' eyelashes and acacia flowers to pass our roast-goat evenings. But I have run away with the idea. You're back home, and I daydreamed myself coming here alone as a silly gesture. Look where I've ended up even in my daydream, drinking beer in the corner of a poorly-conceived hotel room and feeding my hat to insects. *Timbuktutored*, the receptionist might say, who would have seen this all before. *Timbuktoo little Timbuktoo late*, he might add before returning to his crossword.

I'd do anything
For you, dear, anything;
Yes, I'd do anything
[Anything?]

anything

for you but leave my slapdash idea of a metaphorical hotel room and face the city itself, and on the morning of my flight I know I would be woken up by the starlings who would be shouldering the dawn.

Fears and Confessions of an Ortolan Chef

In many ways my workplace is the loveliest in the whole country. They are still songbirds, after all, even when they are screaming in the pot.

You once told me that nobody could ever fall in love with a person whose job involved boiling birds in liquor. I did the usual thing and attempted to romanticise the delicacy of the dish and its traditions. I described the birds as ingredients – the word *gourmand* was used until, in horror at my pretension, you set about tickling it from my vocabulary. You had wanted to move in with someone who made excellent sandwiches and the occasionally impressive dessert but I began to wonder whether I was in danger of becoming something far more sinister in your eyes, all bloodlust and dirty tricks beneath a cloche.

Fear of this made me switch tactic and I began talking about the specific dish in terms of the brandied birds as being like insects trapped in amber or tapped syrup on a tree trunk. You asked whether I ever thought about the words *eau de vie* on the brandy bottle's label and moved to the colder side of the bed. Hungrier and sadder and fatter with love than I have ever been before, I stopped explaining the method by which the meal is cooked and the rituals involved in its consumption and tried to push it from my mind.

The next day I came home stinking of illegal food to find a handwritten list on the kitchen counter. I picked up the piece of paper and read it while you explained we should attempt an experiment or regimen for our first month living together. Grease from work smudged the margins of the piece of paper in my hands and turned its corners translucent. You had compiled a syllabus for us – for a month we only read books that had been banned after publication, we ate unethically and often in bed, and we ignored the DVDs that lay taped-up in our packing crates and instead sought out films that had at some point been censored or outlawed upon release. The content of these films ranged from cannibals to mad doctors to Lloyd George. They were bad for our newly veal-bulky stomachs and *Areopagitca*-bleary eyes.

The kitchen where I work blinds the ortolans and keeps them alive in lightless boxes beneath the sink. According to custom, the birds are then fed on figs every day until they double over, at which time it is my job to drown them individually in Armagnac. There is also a tradition required of those who demand to eat ortolan which involves a certain amount of pomp and prop-cupboards. It is a complete irritation for our waiters and the restaurant's laundry bill. According to the rite each diner should cover his or her head with a large embroidered napkin. Beneath this hood one can bite off the head of the bird and eat its body, bones and all. I sometimes catch glimpses of the customers during the meal through the kitchen doors and they look like they are attending a séance or waiting for their hangmen.

If you are in the know, ours is the restaurant to contact for this banned meal. My friend who works on Reception tells me that most of our bookings are made over the telephone in such hushed whispers that the clients-I-mean-customers-I-mean-guests regularly have to be told to speak up. The orders come flooding in. Our assiduous staff are trained in discretion and how best to evade eye contact when pulling out chairs for our diners and taking their coats. Our restaurant caters for whole groups who seek illicit songbirds. We have a back room that is reserved precisely for parties who order this dish, the only one fitted with a dimmer switch.

The more I think about it, I suppose the meal is not really like a séance or like gallows at all. Although an ortolan is generally eaten in silence, or with a performance of silence that is maintained in order to imply gravitas, you can hear the smacking of lips and groans of enjoyment beneath the napkins. There is a general feel of boardroom shoulder-slapping and people talking about golf over dessert.

As our first month living together drew to an end, I found a spreadsheet on your laptop. You are researching titles of more banned books to read in your own time. I start to think that stealing looks at you while you sleep is like being in a kitchen and knowing where the knives are kept.

I grow sick of metaphor and sick of the idea of the bird. I am certainly sick of having pride in any talent I might possess in terms of the birds' preparation – they are just claws and fluff and hard mouthparts on a plate. I told you once about the day the dishwasher had flooded because some leftovers had worked their way into the machine's filter and clogged the drains. I was nominated to sort out the problem and I spent the night elbow-deep behind the dishwasher, twirling a length of wire along the pipe until I felt something snag. The open-mouthed little head did not meet my eye as I pulled it from the grey water and slough of the sink. As I mopped up and washed my hands I could hear the ortolans beneath the sink sing a little louder as they sensed that I was close.

'I don't capture the birds,' I told you in our early days in our new house as I helped you unpack. 'We pay people to do that.' This clarification seemed important.

'Do you ever think where they come from?'

'I just know ortolan pays the big bucks.'

'Not *ortolan*. Ortolans. The birds sitting in hedgerows and trees. Being a nuisance under cafe tables.'

'We serve goose, not geese. We serve beef, not cows.'

'They're poached,' you say.

'In Armagnac,' I said.

You let me deliver the line and we listened to the sounds of the traffic outside, and when you asked me to leave the room I made my way to the kitchen to make you coffee. When I returned the door was closed. I left the cup outside on the landing, cleaned my hands, went back to the kitchen and unpacked three of your favourite plates from their bubble-wrap and broke them one by one against the kitchen counter.

We certainly make our elite tent-headed diners pay through the nose for the privilege of forbidden food. We buy them from a boy who wears a big silver watch and bright white sneakers. He charges over €150 for each ortolan bunting and brings them to an alley around the back of the kitchen every month, his bag pulsing with birds still fluttering and hop-angry. Before bedding down on our sofa for the night, I checked that there was no dinner grease from the day left glazed against my skin.

As far as I can remember you have only ever appeared in one of my dreams. In the dream I am preparing a fantastic breakfast for you. It was definitely you although I did not recognise the kitchen nor the bedroom to which I brought the plates on a tray. There were ironed napkins on the tray with my initials on them. As you sat up and ate the dish – delicately, fastidiously, gnawing around the bones of the bird with cat-like enjoyment – you did not stop smiling. You kept smiling and kept my gaze even as you licked your plate clean. Your waking diet would never allow this, neither the food nor the gusto, and I remember as you pushed the tray away you ignored the napkins, moved forward beneath the bedclothes and wiped your face clean on my face. The rest is all a little hazy but I do remember that the dream-us then read the paper together for dream-hours under an embroidered coverlet. I remember that I breathed on your feet when you told me that they were cold. You thanked me, and then you looked in my eyes and told me in a strange, high voice that you could not see. You told me that your breath felt on fire. Then you smiled again and passed me the magazine supplements, and I woke up covered in a cold scorching sweat.

When I tell you about this dream you say that you have had a recurring nightmare since we moved in where I come through the door with feathers in my hair and my thumbs stinking of brandy. I then beg you to lead me through what I insist on calling the most important doors of the house. In the dream, I beg you to help me pull all our bed linen, towels and curtains up over my body and hide my face.

I used to think that a beak must be the most brittle part of any face until I caught sight of my eyes in the bathroom mirror. You have started coming home at night with lipstick on your sleeves and catkins in your hair but I do not want to ask. In between your breaths at night I think I can hear the sound of tooth on bone from the day's kitchen. It is louder than any chopping board or dinner gong. Each evening I watch the diners' heads emerge sleek with sweat when they finally remove their napkins. I had forgotten what it was like to feel fine with showing that kind of desire.

This week when the boy with the big silver watch and the sneakers arrives at the arranged time, I will grab his bag from him and rip it apart right there in the alley. The birds that he brings have their wings clipped so will not be able to take to the sky as I would like. As I give the boy a kicking and he gives me a kicking and we grapple together on the ground, fighting tooth and nail by the bins outside the kitchen, the birds will have to scatter along in the gutter of the street.

I'll talk to you about wings tonight rather than hands. I'll mute the radio, take the heat off, put some bottles down and whatever they're marching for or against on the news tonight I will make sure that I'll hold you and sing from dawn until dawn for both our sakes, and for all the little songs I've stopped.

Synaesthete, Would Like To Meet

When I was eight my sister dropped a copy of the *Yellow Pages* on my head. I was too busy retrieving my tooth from beneath the radiator to notice any immediate change but the next day I found that reading the letter *B* caused a green light to flare directly behind my eyes. My mother explained that I must have been staring too long at the magnetic letters on our refrigerator and was associating their shapes with the corresponding colour of the plastic. This could not explain why an ampersand was suddenly a guttering black for me, however, nor why asterisks had become accompanied by a four-second howl.

Neurological synaesthesia is an unwieldy phrase to sprinkle into conversation so I prefer to describe it this way – the part of one's brain concerned with processing sensory information should be like a highly efficient switchboard. Mine is set up as if someone swapped the wires around, took a mallet to the bodywork and went to town with a soldering iron and a big jug of water.

Apparently I'm a very rare case, featured in so many medical encyclopaedias with labelled photos and everything that I've had to hire a publicity agent. Get me. I have a doctor of my very own who is paid by a multinational pharmacy to investigate my case and observe how I cope with it. He tells me that a number of people experience similar synaesthetic aspects – they associate colours with days of the week, for example, or endure specific tastes when they hear certain sounds. My condition, however, is complete. Dawn's light through my curtains stinks, my first cup of tea is an orchestra tuning-up and the sound of birdsong outside my window tastes of rosewater and it is scalding. This reaction to birdsong perhaps best demonstrates the way in which my condition is not at all logical. In chorus the birds taste of rosewater but individually the pigeons' coos are a soda syphon's stream, the starlings taste of double-mint chewing-gum and blue tits' warble comes, weirdly, with the smell and bobbly feel of pork crackling. The number *3* is orange for me while *10* smells of buttered bread, but add them together and – rather than a buttery, citric compaction of the two – seeing *13* provides the sensation of snakeskin drawn against my upper lip.

Glancing at your number pencilled onto this napkin, I read a line of digits that are gawky and spavined, slightly flushed and buzzing like clarinets.

My life is often an unmanageable series of sensations. Other synaesthetes describe their experiences as pleasant while for me it is a constant sensory overload. Back to the switchboard simile, I have it on good authority that when something overloads it tends to crash. Pick up any paperback that uses too many mixed metaphors and that is my day-to-day, with all attempts at clarity squandered by confusing, muddled leaps of imagery. I see fireflies when a tyre screeches, smell fried onions when I step on an upturned plug. In an attempt to process fewer sensations and block out the worst unexpected repercussions of my surroundings, I have taken to wearing tinted shades even when indoors. I'm well aware how daft this looks.

Always wearing shades and looking either wary or disgusted whenever I leave the house can make for quite a lonely existence. This is why I chat online – if I adjust the settings on my monitor so that all text appears a certain shade of grey on a yellow background I don't have to shield my eyes or stuff up my nose nearly so often. Changing the Display Settings like this just takes the edge off. Grey text on a yellow background sounds so clearly to me like snow on a tin roof and smells so strongly of mown grass that all other synaesthetic responses are dulled.

Online dating marked a huge step. At first I found the profile that I created absolutely disgusting. Reading through it, the paragraphs smelled like tar and vinegar and it was full of chewy toothaching words. I had no hope of any response to such a squalid, acrid thing and imagined that anyone to whom it might appeal in any way must have some kind of perversion I did not want to share. You must understand that it was not just that I did not have high hopes – I actively dreaded who would be interested in such a thing. I gave it to my doctor to edit and he gave me two thumbs up, but I could tell by his tweedy, neoprene-edged vowels that he was just being kind.

Your email back, however, smelled like a sea breeze. That was all it took. I didn't have to read about the interests you listed, your hobbies or your star sign. It was that sea breeze smell cutting through the snow sounds and mown grass that convinced me this was a chance I had to take. I organised a meeting.

You chose a spot near Piccadilly in view of Eros and the Criterion. I like Piccadilly Circus. The exhaust fumes and the chatter present me with a fresh inky blue. It's almost precisely the colour of the line on the Tube map. To me the flashing adverts are a barbershop quartet suffering the giggles which makes me smile, and the tourists' inter-braiding accents cause a firework display of neurological responses. The taxi drivers' swearing is accompanied by different shades of silver, squeaky and lickable.

As I waited, the rain made a pink overture against my jacket.

And your colour, when you introduced yourself? You must not be insulted, but you were blank. A soundless, tasteless, brilliant blank.

There was no poetic extension, no misfiring of fizzing neurons as you said your name and shook my hand. I followed you to the cafe and as we spoke our coffee tasted of coffee and when we shared it your cake tasted only, gloriously, of cake. All the unnecessary colour and clamour just drained away – an oil spill's fringe of rainbow fading into pure water. In clarity we swapped numbers and arranged to meet again, and as soon as you boarded your bus all the colours and sounds and smells rushed back at me.

I can tell you that as I watched your bus turn the corner the rain was singing a sweeter, brighter note. It was too sweet, almost, and just a touch too bright.

I mentioned all of this to my doctor in his private clinic the next morning. I told him about you, and the cafe and how all of my senses had come flooding back once you were out of sight. He took notes and looked very sympathetic as I finished and asked what he advised. Irritatingly, he did not seem to want to help me with the etiquette of the situation, however, and as I hunched on the plastic seat he shot me a look that tasted of mackerel and grapefruit. He reached for a fresh pen.

'Nothing at all?' he pressed. 'You suddenly felt everything was back to normal, for a whole afternoon?'

'Everything felt *abnormal*,' I corrected.

'Fascinating,' he said. He looked at his computer and began typing.

'I don't want to feel fascinating,' I said. 'I want to be sure that not –' I tried to pick my words carefully, '– that not having any responses like this isn't some indicator that I'm going to blow a gasket.'

'Brushing up on your medical terminology, I see,' said my doctor. He did not look away from his screen.

'Sarcasm tastes like wet dog,' I said.

'But you felt good,' he continued. 'In that moment, where you weren't being overwhelmed on all sides?'

'It was wonderful,' I said. 'Right up until –'

'And you would want to replicate it?' he said, cutting me off and looking up from his computer.

'Completely wonderful,' I repeated. I watched a few purple spangles above his head spin and pivot in the air. 'And then completely terrible.'

'I see,' said my doctor, and I watched hundreds of puce, winking sequins clot and cluster around his head with genuine concern. He tapped with greater urgency at his keyboard then swivelled on his chair and handed me a piece of paper. 'What are you doing this evening?'

On his prescription pad he had written the names of three films.

Three hours later my doctor was sitting in a red velvet chair next to me with his eyes trained on my face as the trailers started.

'Just pretend I'm not here,' he said. He added in

a half-mutter, 'Can't believe you've never seen *Casablanca*.'

I raised my hiss to aquamarine levels so that he could hear me in the packed cinema. 'Don't you think that by observing me,' I said, 'that you'll affect any response I might have?'

He adjusted the notepad on his knee. It was difficult for him to take notes due to the darkness of the cinema. He had not been able to resist buying a carton of popcorn as we passed through the lobby either and there was not much room on his lap. 'Let me worry about that,' he said, munching and staring at my pupils. He leaned a little closer over the armrest to peer at my face as the first lemon strains of the film's opening titles began.

I did not ask him what he observed about me during the film but as the credits rolled I saw his face shimmering with an unmistakeable diamante haze. He was disappointed. A migraine raspberried in my tear ducts and my brain was ringing.

'Nothing?' he asked. 'None of that – how did you describe it – no clarity?'

'It gave me a headache,' I said. 'The usual kind of headache when everything is all too much.' I didn't know what he wanted me to say. My sinuses were singing with jazzy, slippery blares. 'At times my mind wandered –'

'Yes?' said the doctor, encouraged. I watched him tongue a crumb of popcorn from the corner of his mouth.

'At times my mind drifted,' I said.

'Specify! You were bored?'

'No. It would have drifted whatever the film. This – this is embarrassing –'

'Go on.'

'I just started thinking about yesterday in the cafe. And everything became all jagged.'

My doctor wrote down that I was flushed and agitated and he reached up over his empty popcorn carton to pat my shoulder. From his jacket pocket he handed me two tickets to the opera.

I blinked at him through my headache. 'Why are there two –?'

He interrupted as soon as he saw the route my mind was turning. 'It's for me and you,' he said. '*Intensity*. Emotional immersion!' His tie had slipped into his carton of popcorn. 'We'll try some Monteverdi, and maybe an art gallery. But maybe I'm showing my biases – where can we lose you, do you think?' Such was the pressure of the film's residual sounds and textures I was finding it difficult to keep my eyes open. He interpreted my pause as scepticism, or confusion, or generally as an invitation to continue. 'We won't be able to observe any useful results in a lab so it makes sense to keep you under scrutiny out in the wild.'

This does not seem like a good use of funding, I wanted to say. Or rather, *This all seems like a wonderful use of funding, but all I want to do is return to my computer with its calming mown grass and snow-on-a-tin-roof screen.*

'You could just come along to my next date,' I said. I had a vision of him sitting at a table next to us, his eyes visible through holes cut into his broadsheet newspaper. I imagined your face when I was forced to explain who he was. I imagined your face and began to feel faint.

My doctor cleared his throat.

'I don't think that would be a good idea,' he said.

'No,' I agreed.

His snail-shell tone changed to one prickled with stiff bristles and I realised that I had misunderstood. He did not mean that such an observation would be inappropriate.

'In fact,' he said, and for the first time in the evening he looked away from my face and to the cinema screen, 'I don't think it would be wise to plan another meeting until we're quite sure what's going on. We have no idea what another episode –'

I understood his intentions. When he mentions you I understand he sees you as something of a threat. It might amuse you to know that in all my following sessions with him – whether back in his clinic or in the stalls at the ballet or in the middle of a moshpit as he shouts diagnostic questions and answers over its abrasive sheet of garnet-perfumed sound – he says your name with a certain professional jealousy. I believe that he thinks you might be my chance of a breakthrough and he wants that triumph for himself.

Here is a warning, then, and a too-late apology for my lack of communication. Since our meeting my synaesthesia has become more intense. You should know that when I returned from the cafe on the day that we met, as I pulled the door closed behind me I noticed the semi-quaver of a stray eyelash had settled on my shirt. It was one that you had blown unthinkingly from your finger. Perhaps you do not remember. You should know that this eyelash was the loudest thing I had ever heard and the sound of it almost threw me across the room.

I told my doctor, and to use the words that he committed to his case files with excited exclamation marks: quite literally every thought of you sends me reeling. This is the root of my fear, however – that if we met again you might perform something incidental and catastrophic. I want to message you and politely ask that you do not, for example, tip up on your toes at a second meeting, or let the sun anywhere near your hair. That you won't laugh off-guard, for example, or gnaw at your fist or smooth your palms against your elbows in the way that I noticed, signifying that you are frustrated. And as sure as hell don't you ever again kiss me goodbye because I cannot promise it would not leave me blinded.

Bulk

We were all on the beach for different reasons when we found the whale. The moon was still up and the morning was cold enough that our conversations could be seen writ faintly in the air above our heads as breaths met in the early winter sky. They appeared first as threads from our lips that briefly formed one shape, connective and fragile like a wishbone.

I remember looking at my watch as I approached and saw it was not yet seven o'clock.

I am not too sure how many of us in total were gathered there staring at the whale's body – fewer than ten, let's say. In many ways I am an imperfect eyewitness. I was close enough to have been able to make out all of their features in the bad light, the good dark, but at the time such a thing seemed unimportant. I slipped a little on a hand of bladderwrack as I scuttled over the rocks to join the knot of bystanders on the shoreline.

'Do you think we can push it back?' someone was asking the group as I arrived. Whether out of reverence or an absurd sense that something so big and so dead might be eavesdropping on us, disapproving of our small lives and concerns, we all spoke to each other in eking whispered slivers.

'It's long gone,' came an answer. The man wore stout, expensive, too-clean boots and his vowels sounded well-rested and alert. 'I tried to get closer earlier, and the gulls or the crows have already taken its eyes. I only left for a moment to fetch my camera from home,' he went on, 'but I spotted you all moving in so I thought that I should come back.'

'They drown in air,' said the young woman closest to me. She was carrying a metal flask and leaning against the man on her other side. One could tell immediately that this couple had not yet been to bed and were not entirely sober – they used their hands too much when they spoke and stood swaying in evening clothes that were not doing them favours in the frosty sea breeze. They smiled at each other constantly and shared looks over their shared flask while the rest of us stared ahead at the whale in the water. 'Drown in air?' echoed her young rumpled man, unconvinced and affectionate. 'It happens,' she insisted.

She gnawed on the wool of his jacket.

'*One* of us did well in their biology exam,' he said, and he looked at the rest of us for congratulation. 'Got seventy-six percent! Marks back just last week.'

The young woman, feigning embarrassment, added, 'Out of a hundred,' and then looked around at us too, and pulled the man closer to her side.

As we murmured responses without knowing why, I noticed that another one of our group seemed to be crying. She had a flask in her hands too. No, look again – it was not a flask, it was an urn. Perhaps she thought that this time in the morning would be a good quiet moment to come down to the beach and find it empty enough for her purposes. I patted my pocket for tissues but I had not set out on my drive this morning prepared for whales nor mourners.

'Have you had a drink up there, at the hotel?' the young man was asking me. Some gulls overhead began wheedling and wheeling, making jagged chevrons of the sky with their shoulders. 'The guy behind the bar tried to serve me a Martini with a glacé cherry in it.'

'I live next door to there,' I said in case he had seen me the previous evening and was trying to place my face. He assessed me blearily but closely. He leaned further in, speaking over his companion's hair. 'This one here – I love her so much. I love her loads,' he said, and he squeezed his arm about her waist but kept his eyes on me. I said nothing and he interpreted this as a prompt. His voice was still a whisper and it sang with alcohol. 'She worms into you the way that smoke gets into your hair.' He nodded and would not stop nodding until I nodded too. His eyes dropped to the plastic bag in my hands.

When I first saw the whale from the road, I had pulled over into a lay-by and broken into a run without closing the car door as if I thought that I could be of any possible physical use or as if being the first to the scene might afford me special privileges later down the line. As I made my way along the shoreline I tripped over the remnants of a picnic left among the dunes. There was a newspaper, some bunched tinfoil, a blue plastic bag and an abandoned packet of digestives. I had stopped and tidied the mess together, and noticed that the newspaper's crossword was completed with a thick red marker pen; the clues had been ignored and instead every box was filled with the name *ANNA ANNA ANNA ANNA* both Across and Down. A neat coven of ants had arranged itself around the rim of a discarded biscuit too, headbutting it and worrying at its crumbs. They were working around the biscuit's circumference in a slow-moving country dance. I let them have it and walked over to the people looking at the soft-bucking surf and its whale.

'Is this yours?' I said, shaking the bag, and the man recoiled.

The morning light had a silky, pearly menace to it and I could feel the salt on my lips. Another member came skittering across the rocks to swell our group. He had a small dog at his feet, a wiry, teddybearish breed that looked frayed at the edges. The dog kept to our line and regarded the whale with a very frank expression while the owner comforted the woman carrying the urn.

'We didn't know where you had gone,' he said to her. He looked as if he too had been crying all night.

By now the other man with the stout boots had clocked the urn-holding and as the dog-owner held the woman, stout-boots said something in a low voice that was calculated to be calming. I did not quite hear the beginning of his sentence because the wind changed and a gull gave a loud cry, but watching all three faces involved I knew that he should probably shut up. In the next moment the wind changed again and I heard him conclude, '– and when we scattered him it changed the pH levels in the soil so the next year the hydrangeas were blue instead of pink.' They allowed him to finish, and then the woman with the urn and the man with the dog glared at the stout-booted man so he looked over to meet my eye, then glared at the bag of rubbish in my hand disapprovingly.

'I want to touch it,' the girl in the evening-wear said, and she broke from our line to move towards the body of the whale. The young man pulled her back by the sleeve of her dress, gently – she shook him off, annoyed, but did not advance any further.

'Do you think it's warm?' I heard her ask. 'I can't believe it doesn't smell.'

I was acutely aware of my work lanyard around my neck and, as she spoke, I stowed it away under my jumper.

'I bet it would make this sound if you rubbed it,' said her companion. He made a high-pitched squeaky-honking noise, *whgeehh wheeghh wghheehh*.

'I bet it feels like an aubergine under water when you wash it. When you wash them,' said the woman with the urn. The younger woman took another pull of her flask and the man with the dog dipped his chin beneath his scarf more snugly.

'Like an aubergine,' the drunk man repeated, and we all heard the giggle rising through his line.

'Or like a wellington boot,' said the woman with the urn. After a while in an attempt to break the mood the man with the stout boots and well-rested voice said, 'Last year, someone was throwing a ball for their dog over on those cliffs up there. They were telling me all about it at the hotel bar. Someone was throwing the ball and the dog bringing it back. Throwing the ball, the dog bringing it back. They threw the ball once more and the dog went for it again but they had miscalculated ... the ball went over the cliff edge and the dog just went with it, right over.'

We all turned and looked at the red and white cliffs looming over the beach. They looked like wine-stained teeth and all our footsteps led from them. I could hear my car's alarm alerting me to its open door.

The younger woman stretched out her hand in the whale's direction and traced the outline of it in the air. Her friend kept a grip on her elbow but, sensing that she was distracted, he leaned in closer to me again. His breath was full and wobbly as he inclined his head towards his companion. 'When she paid for the drinks last night,' he said, conspiratorially, 'she used the –' and the man extended his hand out, crooking his fist and demonstrating, '*this* part to punch the number in the machine rather than the tips of her fingers. The knuckles. Punch punch punch.'

'Maybe she's worried about germs,' I said.

'Indicative,' he said unsteadily, and then he reeled his friend in and kissed the top of her head. We all looked back to the whale lying in the surf.

After a few minutes of collective silence, the man with the stout, too-clean boots piped up. 'I have seen dead whales explode on TV,' he said. 'They swell up with the gas caused by the bacteria and then, *boom*!, guts everywhere just showering down. It happens quite often.' This man's voice was very well-to-do and the way that he said the word *often* meant that it would rhyme with *orphan*. Perhaps this was the reason that the drunk couple began openly giggling. It was a beautiful voice – as if the stout-booted man was giving an a cappella of speech, rather than just talking – but it seemed so performed and out of place. The gulls wheeled closer above our heads.

'Are you from around these parts?' the woman with the urn asked the stout-booted man. She seemed to have dried her eyes and was looking a lot better. The dog, sitting now at my feet, kept its nose pointing at the body of the whale with the same rapt expression.

'I'm one of the people living this month up at the bothy,' said the stout-booted man, and he pointed up at the cliffs again. 'Perhaps you've seen the posters.'

'The *converted* bothy,' the woman with the urn corrected him, and the stout-booted man coughed. The drunk couple laughed again into their sleeves. I knew a little about the cottage he meant. Draughty with cold walls and the kind of cheap paper lampshades that look like pale globes or imitation moons or a thin-skinned grub suspended from a wire. I had visited one of the artists there, invited to stay the night after some cleric-collared pints together at the cliff-top glacé cherry hotel. It was a nice enough inside and nice enough company. As I got dressed in the morning, I remember that I had looked out at their view of the sea and at their cocoon-lampshade, and I could not help but think about my beetles waiting for me at work. As I looked again at the whale and followed this thought, I recalled the smooth metal dish that had sat on the bothy's windowsill. The artist in residence at the time had called from their residency by the bed that this dish was a Tibetan singing bowl. They confessed that they had been using the Tibetan singing bowl as an ashtray, and I had thought about my beetles at work again and the clacking of their scales and frass.

'Did you say whales *explode*?' the woman with the urn asked the group. Out of politeness to the stout-booted artist and his facts about whales we all took a step back from the water's edge and its cargo. As they retreated, the sleepless, rumpled couple let their giggles grow louder and the air swelled with the largeness of a laugh and changed the format of the whale-near breeze.

The man with the dog had turned to me and asked me directly. 'Yes. Is that true about the explosions? You'd know all about it, I expect, you being –' and he mimed something that denoted professionalism while also taking in the bulk of the whale with a sweep of his arm. The group's heads all turned to look me at me, to search me up and down. The dog shifted against my shin, embarrassed on my behalf at the attention, and his owner pointed at my neck, presumably at the just-visible purple cord of my lanyard. 'I saw your ID card. You're from the museum, aren't you? Specimens and that.'

I don't know a thing, I wanted to say. *I am not very clever but I am affectionate about knowledge. Let's start there.* I had started driving around the coastal roads at four that morning because I could not sleep for fear of dreaming about the beetles, and I had hoped that the thrum of the engine and the blank, banked hedges of the roadsides would help calm me down or make the idea of my coming day and its silent beetles bearable.

'Natural history museum,' explained the man with the dog to the woman with the urn, and everyone nodded and looked at me again expectantly.

'What should we do?' asked the man with the dog.

'Police?' asked the woman with the urn.

'Ambulance?' asked the girl with the flask. She and her friend and the gulls collapsed again with laughter.

I wanted to tell them that I did have a professional stake in the whale and that I should be the one to call it in. I wanted to tell them that I oversaw the dim rooms on the museum's second floor, rooms that were not open to any visitors and certainly not if visitors were to try to enter carrying urns and flasks and frank-faced little dogs. We keep three beetle colonies there in big glass tanks, I wanted to tell them. The colonies pick apart any organic material that is placed in with them. They surge forward and over and under and through, and strip every scrap away, right down to the bone. It is clean work. It is so much better to use dermestid beetles in this way to whisk flesh and matter from specimens so that they can be prepared for exhibition – it is certainly the quickest and the cheapest method, and boiling can destroy the cartilage.

I wanted to tell them what a gift the sea had given them and I moistened my lips, twisting somebody else's plastic bag in my hands, but the wind changed a third time and I could not bring myself to speak against it. The ill-dressed young man beside me gave a shiver and used his shirtsleeve to wipe his mouth.

When I watch them at work, the movement of my beetles across the specimens seems so fluid and neat. I can't imagine a beetle being cowed by a whale's size and I wondered if the museum would be able to find a tank big enough if the cuts are made the right way. I wondered whether beetles ever suffer from insomnia, or think beetle-thoughts about huge bodies of water with something like gratefulness.

'I *will* touch it!' declared the young woman suddenly with a renewed vigour and she slipped from her partner's arm and ran in an arc out towards the head of the whale, picking out a route over the rocks with shoeless feet. There was an ungainliness about her small size next to the great bulk of the whale. There was an imbalance to the scene on the shoreline generally, as if a note was being sung off-key or somewhere a pair of parentheses had been left unclosed. I had the number that I should call for moments just like this stored in my phone. There are procedures I knew I should be following – I knew that I should look at the whale and see logistics and admin. I thought about the mitral valves that would be exposed, named after the bishop's hat they resemble, and I thought about the sight of actual heart-strings that are as long as your arm, and imagined them being pulled cherry-bright against the bruising water and cloud-damp. I thought about striped chalky cliffs and the texture of the metal bowl hidden up there on a windowsill, sitting with its curled cooling cigarettes lying dusty at its centre.

If I made the phone call, I knew that men and women would arrive in the appropriate branded vans with matching plastic outfits and small logos on the chest. Men and women with saws and chainmail gauntlets on their arms to protect their flesh as they set to work. I thought about the baleen of the whale's mouth, thick as horsehair, and the meat that would be shown to the sky. The fact that this meat would be dark with oxygen, almost black – darker than venison or duck – while the blubber would be a white tinged a pale pink. I know your underbellies, I think, as I looked at the whale and at the watchers of the whale – I know the spread of your systems when they are all laid out and spread on a table or against the rocks. There is a heart there big enough for me to lie upon and sleep and not touch the rocks if I curled up with my knees tucked under my jaw. If the men and women arrive it will take three tractors just to drag the body up the beach and flip it over. I know the procedures involved, I think, and that they might loop a thick chain around the whale's heart once they get to it. The tractors would then have to heave it along the rocks, scrabbling for purchase with their tough treads, along the rocky shore.

I fixed my eyes on the whale in the water and continued to pass the blue plastic bag between my hands. The gulls made their thoughts clear on the matter and waited for my answer. Above us and above the gulls, the morning's just-visible moon pulled the sea an inch inwards as if for a waltz.

Platform

On Platform One a businessman's toupée was caught by the wind and blown smack-bang into another commuter's face. I was opposite on Platform Two when this happened taking a photo of my friend leaving me forever. I did not notice the toupée incident until a month later when I had ordered the photo of my friend to be developed and blown up into a poster for my wall. You can do that nowadays. In the poster, the ticket stub for the train journey pasted up next to it on my wall, my friend's face is about two inches tall. That is around the same size as a satsuma if you step back about a foot away from the poster and hold up a satsuma. A lime is too small for this exercise.

In magnifying the picture, not only was the figure of my friend leaving me forever made a great deal bigger but the people beyond were similarly scaled-up.

I was in the process of trying to forget you when I noticed the men and women on Platform One in the background. Seven out of the nine cars that had passed my house that day were red (your favourite colour) and the other two were blue (the colour of your eyes). Earlier in the week I was eating a bowlful of Alphabet Soup and I swear the letters I dragged out that made anagrams of your name tasted sweeter. The woodpigeons were cooing your name outside my window every morning and the fabric conditioner that you use had leaked somehow into the daisies and the dandelions and the crocuses (you are not here any more to remind me that the plural should be *croci*, because you have gone, forever) so the air was heavy and milky with the smell of your laundry. Your laundry was also in the buddleias and pushed about by bumblebees into begonias in the park, clogging up the pansies in the hanging baskets. It was in the daffodils on my garden path, the marigolds on my garden path. My garden path's dead leaves were full of it and so was the snow in the winter. Then it was in the daffodils all over again.

It took a year of standing in front of this poster with satsumas in my hands and your fabric conditioner in the buddleias before I realised the drama that was unfolding behind you in the poster.

I don't remember the day you left forever being particularly windy but according to any toupée-based Beaufort scale it must have been rattling about at quite a bluster. In my photo the toupée has been caught suspended halfway between the two men like a ridiculous Frisbee of hair, or one of those gliding squirrels – a morbidly obese one that is flat with no hands or feet. I have since looked up these flying squirrels: Latin name *Glaucomys volans*, a fact that sends my mind in all sorts of directions. *Glaucomys*, glaucoma, mud in your eye or the wool falling from your eyes, scales lifting from them.

But – the toupée.

I must say I am glad I do not have to worry about wearing one of those. I tried to imagine where the businessman might keep it at home when it was not in use. I think I would make a celebration of it, prop it upon a velvet cushion with tassels or have it balanced on some kind of gilt dais that would rise every morning by my bedside before I began my toilette.

Does he have one toupée for mornings, one for evenings? One for weddings, one for funerals? A Sunday best toupée? In the poster on my bedroom wall there are some pigeons on Platform One that have puffed themselves up in spring-eagerness to mate. They are eyeing the toupée with a mixture of horror and lust.

Why would this commuter, clearly unwilling to embrace his baldness, choose a toupée and not a comb-over? Presumably a comb-over requires a long cat-flap of hair if one is to smear it over-and-across your scalp. *Smear* is judgemental language. I should check myself. I wondered whether there was some brand of specific glue for toupées or whether an individual's hairpiece simply required a snug, moulded fit? He must have gone, then, to a fitting. I feel the sides of my own head, cupping my skull's brow and crown and arch and I am not sure whether mine would be a Small, Medium, Large, EXTRA LARGE. Or would it be measured as an A, a B, C, D, Double D, a Gamma Minus? What are the units of head size: cubic inches? Millilitres?

And would one put the fastening glue on the lining of the toupée (do they have linings?), or is it a Velcro system, or sticky-back plastic? It occurred to me that should I ever be strung up upside down by my toes (like the Hanged Man tarot card, or Mussolini) not only might the spare change fall from my pockets but my toupée might fall off. A whole new world of neuroses right there.

I stood back from the poster.

I reasoned that this commuter resented his full and luxuriant beard and dreamt of the day the follicles there would flee his chin, uproot and migrate upward through his flesh and across his scalp.

What was that monkish bit at the back of your head called? Your pate. Pate looks like pâté when written down. That could result in all kinds of bother, I thought to myself, all sorts of hi-jinks and misunderstandings: 'I need a toupée for my prematurely balding pâté.'

I stood back from the poster of you on Platform Two and wondered what else there was being covered up, up and away that I could not make out from my photograph. False hair, false teeth, false eyes in their heads, false legs in their shoes, false train-times on the walls, false words in their mouths. Tattoos doodling fake signs onto skin (does tattooed skin make coloured dust? Could the commuter have tattooed a full head of hair onto his pate and got around the problem that way?). I put down the satsuma and came closer to the poster so that my breath bounced back at me, heavy and grey against its surface gloss. I ran a finger over the Starbucks-laden women pushing their prams, their mother-and-child faces plugging identical sippy cups. I tried to remember the sounds of that station a year ago. Men and women talking on mobile phones and the mad Voice of God transport-tannoy hallooing from on high with its platform alterations.

The toupéed commuter was mortified. That much was clear from his expression. I could see his face turning red – the print-resolution of the poster and its attendant pixellation made his face a rhubarb-and-custard swirl of embarrassment.

That bright day on the station in spring I was thinking about you leaving and also of gravity, eyeing my shoelaces' angle to the yellow MIND THE GAP lines and looking at the dull rails and the bright rails on the tracks. I was close to rocking upward on the balls of my feet and pitching forwards. Instead, I took that picture as a bald man blustered a bit on a station. A train pulled in, you hopped aboard, and I went home to a house where the pigeons have only now a year later stopped shouting your name.

Rosette Manufacture

A Catalogue & Spotters' Guide

For our purposes the word *rosette* refers to those badges that are worn by candidates or supporters to indicate their political affiliation. These badges are often ribboned. Our rosettes are manufactured according to party colours and many feature the name of the specific party or bear the party's logo at their centre.

Traditionally, rosettes do *have* a colour and are phenomenal rather than noumenal decorations. This is on account of the pin. The pin is the thing. Without a pin, a rosette might look like a synthetic wreath in your buttonhole, which would be ridiculous.

All our rosettes are handmade and we pride ourselves on the fact that each one is sewn up and not glued. This ensures that all our rosettes are made to the highest possible quality.

The silent stink of our pins can push right through a lapel if the correct force is applied – through a shirt-front and on through whatever taut softness lies beyond that so that in this way the rosette can ink straight into the heart and enter the bloodstream, reach the lining of the gut and its thornless little flora, and onwards into the very nerves of it – the body – or sluice all the way to the top of the head and other outliers such as the index finger and the thumb and all the silly muscles that are required to hold a pencil.

We have also supplied rosettes to international dog shows (specifically all-breed championship dog shows, agility dog shows and obedience dog shows) as well as bird show rosettes, gymkhana rosettes, dressage rosettes, riding club rosettes and pony club rosettes.

As skeuomorphs of diminutive spiny flowers, the concept of rosettes relies on pricking. Let us say that we made our rosettes in a garden. We would have to be careful when harvesting them in case the stems prick us so might use long-handled swinging blades. The noun *scythe* always sounds rather negative and needlessly aggressive and we would have to work on the wording to make the cut-backs sound persuasive. Similarly, when discussing drafts of any accompanying literature it is important that terms like *backstroke* should be used rather than *forward slash*.

Sweeping the nation and using only the highest-quality woven-edged polyester ribbon, we might consider branching out and painting rosettes that are expressly intended for loved ones and/or dead-heading. We might paint them in other gardens while singing in a looking glass with some yellow flamingo-canaries that are bent into croquet mallets and are lined up in the background, propped against the scenery. There might be crooked blue trees in this garden and little red-breasted things making small noises above our heads and beneath us – we would tend the trees as well as the rosettes so that we might later manufacture paper and papers as a side business. We would feed the bees and the birds protein-rich bonemeal and so on. There might be lots of small grey columns in the garden for tasteful, obscure landscaping reasons, and a bright yellow and purple puddled heap in the garden that we can only think was the result of too much Berocca® and beetroot the night before.

On a screen in this rosette garden, men might be joking about hats and a woman might paste a honeycomb pattern on something that looks like a crumbling spine. Look at that instead. Numbers might come in as we dismantle the trellises and frames, and the surfaces in the garden might swerve and glitch as if overrun by aphids. It's all a bit much. Let's put a pin in this garden.

Those who invest in horticulture will know that the word *rosette* can refer to a circular arrangement of leaves whereby, from a certain angle, all of the leaves appear at a similar height. Things can be deceiving, and tact comes into play. According to the appropriate lore, 'rosettes often form in perennial plants where the upper foliage dies back so that the remaining vegetation protects the plant [...] part of the protective function of a rosette, like the dandelion, is that it is hard to pull from the ground; the leaves come away easily while the taproot is left intact.'

Rosette is also the word given to certain markings that can be found on the fur of some animals. These are distastefully ribbonless, non-handmade blotches really. These animals do not appear in obedience dog shows nor gymkhanas and might include jaguars, leopards and some lion-tiger hybrids. Their rosettes do not change, idiomatically. There is little craft to their rosetterie nor any associated guidelines as per their cultivation. One can read elsewhere that these rosettes exist 'either as a defence mechanism or as a stalking tool. Predators use their rosettes to simulate the different shifting of shadows and shade, helping the animals to remain hidden from their prey.' Flush the jaguars from your garden and buy your rosettes in bulk in trusty polyester!

The pricking is the thing. The pinning down is the thing.

Rosettes are corsages pinned down rather than exchanged as a handshake might be cf. smiles, sighs, horror or other lapel-less things. We emphasise that the act of pinning down is crucial. We'll ride in on your tails, we'll pluck at your sleeve, we'll buttonhole you with our jaguar breath.

When pinning down, don't worry about the fabric. If unsure, a popular way to open a pin features the parts of the hand that are used when picking up a pencil.

Sometimes – and not even in very high winds – the plastic false-silk ribbons that depend from a rosette overlap one another and it looks as if a cross or a wavelength or a gene or many other lapel-less things have appeared above your heart.

According to polling stations' rulebooks only the candidates and their agents may wear a rosette. The associated Electoral Commission does not specify any strict rosette dimensions to which one ought adhere but 2008 guidelines do set out a maximum width of 'three to four inches'. There is little comment on length. Endless rosettes. Longer than a tongue (note: rosettes can be a choking hazard). Their ribboned edges can be ruffled and fold in on themselves so that they resemble a Viennetta or something collapsing or the circular folds of those winding, wavering cul-de-sacs that project out of or notch into the lumen of the small intestine. Gutlessness and gutsiness! Rosettes for all and whoops all around!

We will never resign nor leave you. We will go on making our false flowers for non-lovers with the jaguars and monsters for you, in our false garden, in the shade.

Scutiform

I have started wandering around the museum during my now vacant breaks. I have developed a little route or routine and make sure that I pass three specific works in a particular order. Each time I nod at them as I go past as if we are fellow, familiar commuters during a busy day.

The first exhibit is found on the ground floor. She has neither head nor arms, marble drapery sticking to her as if she has just escaped some frat boy's wet T-shirt contest. Her foot is resting upon a tortoise – he might have had races to run or hares' egos to deflate but the goddess is clearly having none of it. Aphrodite Ourania and her club-footed friend. I told you that I had been hurt before and that the experience had toughened me, made me uncaring. *Carry your shield on your back, or return on it* is my motto, I had said to you having memorised the phrase when a previous partner said it to me. At the time I had been appalled and impressed at the pretension. I warned myself that I could leave at any time. You rolled your eyes then made a shape in the air with your hands, drawing an invisible line or cusp of something around me and then tapped the centre of my forehead. I had no idea what you were doing but I went with the touch and rocked a little on my heels. Shields can also serve as coracles. That same evening we swung by a screening of *Blade Runner*. During the bit with the Voight-Kampff test when the interviewer character says *You're in a desert, walking along in the sand* – you had reached for my hand in the darkness.

Tortoise shares the same etymology roots as *torture* and *torment*. I convinced myself that passers-by were laughing at us, that you could bear walking with such a squat, conch-backed plod. The shell is fused to the ribcage which holds the heart. Everything felt soft because it was split or calloused from moving too fast or fleetfooted, hermetically sealing over – I felt we both swallowed our heads into our body. The locomotion of tortoises is mechanical and lumbersome. They are ludicrous fossilised meringues. Tortoises look like nothing less than those small brown upturned UHT milk cartons that everyone can pick up for free in the museum's cafe but never do.

The second exhibit that I always make sure to visit when in the museum is titled *Young Neapolitan Fisherboy Playing with a Tortoise*. The figure is naked and wears a hat. Either I let my guard down or you got under my skin – whichever, I thought solely in awful lines of poetry during those days: *Let's lie here arm in arm, let's get lyrical, let's make psalteries of each other's inexpert mouths*. You were taller than me and in order to get anywhere I often had to lift my chin. That sounds more delicate than the action deserved – I had to crane my neck. I felt impervious and brave, wonderfully dunderheaded with love like the best of them and so many smiles started with you. I was idiot-beamy and bumble-gaited, could barely string a walk together let alone a sentence – I started waking up knowing that beneath the brickwork of my skin my heart had become built like a ziggurat. Our days were glossy and embossed. I remember this every time that I pass this second sculpture in the museum. The statue shows a boy tickling the tortoise's face with a reed. Postcards of this statue sell well.

The third exhibit is a small bronze god – 'identified by notches on the ankles for the wings,' can be read on the explanatory note nailed to the wall. The god looks miserable but I love the way that they are portrayed with hands reaching out ('holding a lost object,' states the caption, 'probably a tortoise').

When the weather is good I take my coffee outside and watch the clockwork-footed tourists in the museum courtyard and imagine my exhibits – secure on their plinths or nailed into their display cases – watching me with their blank eyes through the windows. During the course of a day the shadows cast by their tough stony bodies must twist right around their fixed points. When the hour's right, the shadows might reach right across the museum's bare, bright, white floor.

Mischief

He is a rat trained to detect landmines. He has an excellent sense of slapstick.

My eye is right by him. Below him, really – I should learn to be more precise about these things. Precision and prepositions are important in this business. I am looking up at him as he tests the air with his trip-ready tipmost. *Precision.* I mean his nose. The things I could tell you about the underside of a rat's chin if only I had the right words for their importance! There is much to be learned in his rascal angles, his Buster Keaton cameos. I keep my eye fixed on his profile as I slide my shoulder and my own face – all the silly, hot-damp, unwhiskered inches of it – across the ground and through this red dust so carefully.

Carefully.

We're talking a crumbling, friction-burn tickle kind of carefulness. Meanwhile my rat is all pronk and swagger. His movement is rat-levity – he does a funny walk as I eye the landmine to help relieve the tension. I am well-versed in rat humour so forgive him as I slide in the scrubland's dust and long-gone war grit, my body oblique and still getting the gist.

Timing is very much of the essence *etc.*

In times of stress my mind always wanders. *Keep it together*, I say to my rat. I find that out in the desert my words wander too because here thoughts and words are things unleashed. Also, if I'm honest, I spend far too much time talking only to rats. You may not know this but rats enjoy ungainliness of scansion over content when it comes to speech. I am under no illusions – my charges appreciate the clicks and gurgles that I can produce in my silly, hairless throat far more than any sense I might be making. Lying here with my hand loosely on his tether and sliding inch-slow through the dirt towards the device, I find that I am saying the word *etcetera* to my rat in order to break the mood. My breath makes dust particles dance between us. I watch him boggle with joy at the word *etcetera* and its spokey consonants and rhythms, its bitedowns. This is our workplace banter. Minefield as open-plan office. We'll come back to that – we've come down to that. My timing is all over the shop. For the moment, however, thought-wander a little longer with me as you thank your lucky stars and just *look at that*, will you take a good long *look* at those *whiskers*, dear *Lord*. There's a faceful of well-deployed em dashes to make you weep in the desert. I am a long way from home, specifically its greens and its greys, its slate and its church bells. I resent the fact that snatches of schoolbook scripture always return to me when I'm out in the field, crawling and looking up at my rats' chins from impossible angles. Maybe this means that I'm praying? But I'm just saying *keep it together* and *etcetera* to a rat that I have trained to smell TNT. The bit of the Bible currently lodged in my head runs, jumps, scans something like this: *My brother Esau is an hairy man, but I am a smooth man*. That won't save me, I think – not even that pernickety *an hairy* – and I find that I am wetting my lips. The classroom bibles back home had uniformly blistered blue, plastic covers.

My rat gives a little twitch on his tether and I murmur the word *Esau* to him with hopes of calming him. He preferred *etcetera*, I can tell.

With my face like this in the singing, singeing dirt I'm looking up at him at such close quarters that proximity provides a false perspective. The thin film of dust on the landmine's surface is a mountain range with its own bouldered desert. From down here his whiskers are as thick as a rainbow. Rainbows aren't thick, of course, but despite this rainless place I am put in mind of rainbows of all things because just *look* at the way the sun hits his fur right there, and his filaments, and his learning – there's something about the skittered light and its dazzle-mad-miracle glare against his rat-texture. It seems taut like a rainbow, doesn't it? Wonderful as a rainbow. I remember the day when a triple rainbow looped over the schoolyard back in far-off home. It had scared the daylights out of me. From this angle and appearing so close and huge my trained rat is an ancient god or a planet or a curse. He's a total dreamboat. He's vaudeville and a matinee idol, this guy. He'd suit Footlights I think as my trained rat checks the air and my fingers flatten across our landmine's surface.

When someone first told me that rats could be trained to sniff out landmines, I think it is fair to say that I boggled. Do you know about *boggling*? It is a term used to describe the movement of a rat's eyes when they vibrate rapidly in and out of their sockets. Rats do this when they are content. More on that later. Do you know any good rat jokes? It looks obscene, boggling. It doesn't seem right that eyes should be able to do that. Sometimes rats boggle while grinding their teeth, an action known as *bruxing*. Boggle & Brux, Dickensian attorneys or a disappointing double-act. You wouldn't believe some of the vocabulary that I had to learn while training! And who is learning now, inching and pinching dirt away as gently as possible beneath his current rat-look. I tell you, the silt on the mine looks like a tiny desert.

He is a good rat this one, one of the very best. Light enough to run over the mine and not trigger it with his footfall. These books have soft blue plastic covers. My fingertips are pretending to be wise and there is sweat falling in my eyes. My rat is licking his paws. Perhaps I am praying again beneath my breath but, no, I am just remembering more words from the Bible with useless accuracy – Job 39:25's *At the blast of the trumpet it snorts, Aha! It catches the scent of battle from afar*. Trust me to remember the bit of the Good Book that contains an *Aha!* at a moment like this. My rat yawns at the end of my tether and I have two fingers, decidedly, on the rim of the mine.

I said that this rat has an excellent sense of slapstick and God forgive me I know there is nothing worse than anthropomorphising, except having your face so close to a mine that your eyelashes could graze its maker's mark, so,

give over, and!
this rat, *hell*!

He really knows how to milk a scene. Get a load of this hairy man. If this rat could laugh in a way that you could hear it would be just like the idiom, like a drain – thickly, with gurgles and an undeniable filthiness.

Aha!

Their collective noun is a *mischief* for a reason – I regularly scold the rats back at the training lab with this cleverness of faux-grammar while they do pratfalls from my shoulders and stage chwerthin-chuntering, cheeky-peering productions of *Pyramus and Thisbe* between my ankles. Silly, silky, ridiculous godheads who like it when I say *etc* sternly and forget how to think straight.

This rat with a special yen and talent for slapstick watches me and bruxes. I hope he believes in me with something like a fondness as I pull my hand with its clever thumbs across the metalwork of the landmine. Who is the straight man here, in our pair, and who the fall guy? The term *comic foil* comes from a passage in the Bible.

I made that up.

Rat me out.

The term *foil* in this sense comes from the practice of storing gems in metallic sheeting so that the gleams and glitters of a precious stone might be exhibited to best effect. Did I make that up? *She is more precious than rubies, and all the things thou canst desire are not to be compared unto her.* I wish I knew how to pray better, I think, as my grip tightens minutely. In my hand the rat-tether slackens, minutely.

Our rats begin their training in their fourth week of life. I've personally raised this little mite, this godhead, this little tiny boy with a heigh-ho the wind and the rainbow from when he was but the size of a jelly bean. And now look at him! Now look at him looking at me crying with indecisiveness. Now look at him preen at a good job done well as my hands attempt an untrembling, plucking at a man-made trap in this poor soil so far from home. This rat has Hardy haunches but sighs like a Laurel. As I lie in the dirt he stands over me in such a way that I can see the sun through his ears and I am put in mind of stained glass.

A passage from my training slips in amongst the Bible verses. I didn't understand its significance at the time and yet there it is, tugging at my brain's sleeve. Perhaps you have heard of nominative determinism? The idea is that a person's given name can play a significant part in shaping particular aspects of their profession or character. Someone with the surname *Butler* might be drawn to the service industry, for example, or a *Mr Love* might find some form of amorousness – sought, exhibited, demonstrably withheld, etc – becomes a predominant feature of their life. *Dominique Dropsy* was a goalkeeper in the 1978 World Cup, and together *J W Splatt* and *D Weedon* authored a scientific paper about incontinence for the *British Journal of Urology*. You get the picture. My rat is yawning again. Stay with me. My hands are on a landmine.

Jaak Panksepp.

When I saw this name written down in the training manuals it struck me that it had all the phonetics of a rodent's laugh. *Jaak Panksepp*. In its vowels and cadence I could detect whiskers nudging back in rat-mirth and sleek jaws tugging open with the width of a chirrup. I read about Jaak Panksepp's discovery that when rats played with one another they emitted ultrasonic chirps. These chirps could be *directly associated with a positive emotional state*. Rats laugh! Boy oh boy! *Jaak Panksepp!* And they are ticklish! I am completely disarmed!

I count down from seven – why not seven? – and swallow. I watched my rat breathing in time with me mere inches from my face. I know he cares so deeply about timing and the element of surprise. Dust did what dust does and the sun swelled and swelled, playing its part. I flicked the appropriate mine-things to mine-flick.

'Question,' I say, and my rat looks at the sun and pretends not to hear. My throat is dry, the back of my neck is wet and every breath between us is swinging back and forth like a shared limerick. 'What did the rat say when his friend broke his front teeth?'

My rat blinks as if to say that he is embarrassed for me.

The answer is hard cheese!!!! None of us in the training centre dare to admit that we name our rats because we cannot afford to be sentimental. But between me and you and the landmine and the sky, this rat is my favourite. He has a notch in his ear. He would not unsuit the name Esau. Since our base started operating in this former warzone, rearing and training and spreading the word, our rats have helped detect more than 100,000 active and inactive landmines. That's so many nonsense verses muttered under breath to calm each other, so many nonsense words and rat-laughs, *wifflechop* and *mazyflank*, so many *etceteras* and so much dust. We have over one hundred mine-detection rats accredited at our base and ready to go into the field, and you better believe I print off a certificate each time that one of our guys or gals passes muster. The rats like the sound of the printer in the office when I make these certificates. *Etcetera*, it says to them through a mouth filled with hot ink. *Etcetera*, etc, *boom boom*!

I have so many treats in my pockets. I have so many fingers on the lip of this device. My rat gives me a look that reminds me of Harry Secombe. My rat gives me a look that reminds me of St. David in my school chapel's stained glass. My rat gives me a look that reminds me of music halls and classroom bibles and I cannot thank him enough as I sprawl and let my fingers find the right flavour of purchase on the device.

'Esau,' I say. He boggles at me because I have treats in my pocket.

'Easy,' I say to the landmine.

'I say I say I say,' I say to my rat and he gives a little exasperated floof of cheek for my trouble, encouraging me. 'Where do you go to replace a rat's tail?' I am not nervous when I am out here because I trust my students.

He blinks at the sun once more.

A re-tail store!!!!

'Esau, my hairy man,' I say as my hand stretches full across the landmine's surface. 'Why do rats need oiling?'

And my rat looks at me and the angle of his chin changes in a way that only I could ever understand. A breeze brings glad tidings across our faces as both of us agree that now is not the time to provide punchlines – there is a click somewhere and I cannot speak of squeaking and luck when we are both between rocks and hard dusty places like this, tethered to each other and outstaring our chances in the dirt beneath so open and boggling a sky.

Spines

Michael had argued against buying a cover for the swimming pool from the very beginning. As he explained to his family whenever the subject was broached, he made sure to emphasise that he had just bought them a holiday cottage in an enviable location a mere two hours from Toulouse – the last thing he wanted to add to the bill was a synthetic twenty-foot blue eyelid that would spoil the view and fill up the garden space.

The real reason for Michael's resistance stemmed from the pleasure he derived when scooping the swimming pool clear of insects and leaves every early summer morning when the family stayed at the cottage. Dredging specks and debris from the pool while the rest of his family were still asleep provided a real, ever-replenishing source of satisfaction for Michael. The gunk and flotsam appeared overnight and every day he was able to sweep it aside. He felt that he could now complete the task in a way that was both economic in energy and graceful in execution, dragging the long-handled net across the length of the pool in level, practised arcs. The movement felt good. On the few occasions that the net struck the bottom of the pool, Michael endured a gentle jarring shock across his teeth that he found gratifying. Once the pool was bare he would stand back, shake the contents of the net on to the lawn and admire the freshly-scalped blue water with such pride you might think that the pool, garden and cottage beyond was a scene he had just painted.

Just as this pool-clearing had become her husband's private summer ritual, Jessica's holiday habit was feigning sleep as Michael crept from their bed. She would then steal to the window and watch him at his task. Each year it struck Jessica that the French sun did fine things to Michael's forearms and brought out new colours in the flicks and swivels of his hair.

From Jessica's window as she squinted in the fresh Tuesday morning sunlight, a hedgehog, a small apostrophe in the water, made its way along the side of the pool.

She noticed the hedgehog only a few seconds after Michael. He had ceased his dredging and was looking at the water.

'Is that a rat?' she called down.

Michael's glasses flashed hot and blank up to their bedroom window. 'Of course it's not a rat.'

'Get it out!' Jessica said and she pulled her pyjamas more tightly about her.

Michael squatted down by the poolside. The hedgehog was causing a line of ripples to crimp the pool's even surface.

'It's not a rat,' he repeated. He raised his voice. 'I wouldn't just stand here and let a rat swim in my pool.'

Jessica did not move from the window. 'Just heft it into the rosemary.'

From what Jessica could see, the hedgehog seemed bent on swimming along the pool's circumference. Its snout occasionally hit the ceramic tiles – this contact only served to punt the hedgehog a further inch into the centre of the pool.

Michael straightened. The sunlight glared across the metal pole in his hands and threw a neon fuzz across Jessica's line of sight. 'It'll figure how to climb up the side in its own time,' he said, and he turned away to continue dredging up at the other end of the pool.

Jessica had a long shower and put up her hair. She noticed that there was already a band of pleasingly paler skin visible beneath her watchband, the early litmus test of good holiday weather. She tugged the bed linen into something approaching neatness and folded her and her husband's unmatching pyjamas under their designated pillows. Knowing her son did not like to be woken during the holidays much earlier than lunch, Jessica made her way to the kitchen. Bananas were already fading to a manila brown in the fruit bowl and the tomatoes on the sideboard had developed tired dewlaps and paunches. She binned them both.

The outside air smelt of dried grass and Jessica swatted a wasp away from her still-wet hair. She looked at the swimming pool. The hedgehog was trying to find purchase on the sheer lining and its progress along the poolside seemed to have slowed.

'Can't you fish it out?' she asked Michael again. He was eating a plum and she noticed a bright vein of juice falling along his arm.

'I need to oil the lawnmower,' he said.

'Now?'

The day progressed and the hedgehog kept swimming. A group of curious swallows, dark-uniformed and peak-capped like little *gendarmerie*, began flitting from the sky to drink at the pool. They veered away mid-swoop in perfect formation from the unexpected, prickled smudge trailing across the water's surface.

Without a word to Michael who was clanking and swearing in the outhouse, Jessica laced her trainers and went for a walk to the nearest village. The roads were raw and dusty and all the neighbouring fields and hillsides rusted over with sun. Roadside blackberries were scorched and had grown tarry on their brambles. Rather than clearing her head as she had hoped, the hour-long walk only made her sticky and irritable.

'The bakers' was shut,' she announced to the poolside upon her return. Her son Jamie had risen from his bed by now and was in the pool, hooting and splashing in a pre-lunch swim. Jamie was freshly teenaged and tanning faster than either Michael or Jessica. He shouted louder than his parents had in years. For a moment, still slightly dazed from the walk and noon heat, Jessica felt startled by the sight of him.

'I've already bought some croissants for tomorrow,' Michael said as his wife drew closer to the house. He was wearing sunglasses now and seemed to be enjoying his book. 'I cycled there while you were showering.'

'I needed crusts,' Jessica replied. The hedgehog was in the middle of the pool, turning small circles. 'Do you think croissants count as crusts?' Michael put down his book. 'I thought that we could tempt it out with milk and bread crusts,' Jessica went on. She touched the side of her head. 'That's what we used to give hedgehogs when I was small. Crusts and milk in a little green saucer – we had to shoo the neighbours' cats away every five minutes.'

'That's precisely what you're not supposed to feed them,' Jamie said.

He was treading water and seemed completely oblivious to the hedgehog caught in the wake of his strokes. No doubt his father had explained the situation. Jamie was not very good at keeping afloat and his chin kept slipping under the water so that his eyes were on the same level as the hedgehog.

'There was a big public campaign about it. You're supposed to buy special dog food.' Jamie threw himself into a handstand underwater and blew water out of his mouth in big plume as he surfaced. He smiled at her.

In times of panic, hedgehogs instinctively curl up into their spines to ward off potential predators. The hedgehog did this now. The small brown ball sank a couple of inches towards the pool floor. Michael, Jessica and their son watched as, a moment later, the natural impulse to take a breath caused the hedgehog to uncurl underwater and to bob back up to the surface. It looked like it blinked. This happened twice within a minute. The third time, on the way down, the hedgehog vomited something white and gluey into the water. Jessica began to move towards the pole but Michael caught her wrist.

'If it thinks we'll scoop it out each time, it won't learn,' Michael said. There was a rainbowed thumbprint of grease over one eye of his sunglasses. 'Look, there it goes swimming off again. It'll get the gist.'

'There's another one watching,' her son said from the pool. He pulled a disgusted face as the hedgehog resumed its dogged, blind strokes in his direction. Jamie pointed to the blanched poolside shrubs and if Jessica strained her eyes she thought she could see the tip of a snout there between the leaves. She returned her eyes to the thumbprint on her husband's glasses.

'They're *supposed* to be nocturnal,' Jamie continued. 'That was in the same programme as the dog food information.'

'That one might be its mate,' Jessica said.

'They're not swans,' Michael rejoined, taking his book up again. 'I don't know if hedgehogs go in much for exclusivity.'

'I didn't know France had hedgehogs,' said Jamie, 'let alone that they popped up in the summer. For all we know, that other one over there could be laughing at it. Either way, it's gross.'

Jamie hoisted himself from the pool in a single, glossy rush of movement and began towelling himself down. Jessica came around to help him, pushing his hair into jutting, slick peaks. He was almost old enough to start feeling embarrassed by this contact and Jessica felt him shrug away a little with each pull of the towel.

'They're basically vermin,' said Michael. He was looking over his glasses at his book. 'They probably have rabies or leprosy or something, and Jamie will get Lyme's disease swimming with it. Where's the lilo, Jamie?'

'Only nine-banded armadillos and humans can contract leprosy,' said Jamie.

'You watch too much television,' said his father.

The hedgehog, its back webbed in sick, recommenced its silent circuits.

Jessica went indoors to cut bread.

* * *

It grew too hot to sit comfortably outdoors so when the time came, the family ate lunch at the kitchen table. Salt was shaken, pepper was ground and three types of local mustard were dabbed in gauche sweeps against the bright red napkins. As usually happened every holiday in the cottage, post-meal the family grew sluggish with heat and tense with potentially wasted time – their books were read, restlessly, flies were flapped away and small, terse naps were taken with the shutters closed against the sun. The long-wave radio gave its sports results and topical quiz shows in curdled and echoing English. French rap edged in with occasional unwarranted blurts and pops unless Jamie held the antenna above his head.

'The forecast said it would be too cool this evening for shorts,' Michael said to no one in particular. His paperback was rolled in his fist as he watched a fly on the microwave. 'They sell trousers in the supermarkets here, don't they?'

As he cycled into town the gravel of the drive spat a trail of grit behind his wheels and Jessica went to fish the hedgehog from the pool. Michael had locked the net in the outhouse and she could not find the key. By the time her husband returned, Jessica did not remember to ask him about it. They went back to their books.

* * *

In the cool of the evening the family returned to the pool-side with tea-lights and vinaigrette and they ate omelette with salad and avoided speaking about the weather. Michael had swapped his shorts for linen trousers. While Jessica went back inside to fetch dessert, her husband broke the silence to say he would wait until morning before he removed the two, still hedgehogs floating in the pool.

The water of the pool seemed dim and gentle in the twilight and the hedgehogs were right in the very centre, sitting like asterisks, like parodies of stars.

Spins

SPIDER. *n. ſ.*
[*Skinner* thinks this word ſoftened from ſpinder or ſpinner, from ſpin; *Junius*, with his uſual felicity, dreams that it comes from *σπιδειν*, to extend; for the ſpider extends its web. Perhaps it comes from ſpeiden, Dutch, or ſpyden, Daniſh, to ſpy, to lie upon the catch. *Dor, ðora* Saxon, is beetle, or properly a humble bee or ſtingleſs bee. May not the ſpider be ſpy dor, the inſect that watches the door?] The animal that ſpins a web for flies.

– Dr. Johnson's *A Dictionary of the English Language* (1755)

A tip (Difficult) for users: when choosing the right word to shout at a departing figure, concentrate on exactly how much your throat can handle.

The door slammed behind you an hour ago which means I must have been sitting on the bed like this for just a smidge over two. I've only now noticed the spider up on the ceiling there, however, Miss Muffetting a ragtime beat untimidly above the curtain-rail. It looks as if it is making come-hither gestures at me. Valiant, I throw the closest thing to hand directly at it. The closest things to hand happen to be your pyjamas which you had forgotten to pack.

Aphaeresis is thc process whereby a word loses its initial sound or sounds. *'Twas* and *knock* are two examples. Sounds are lost from the ends of words through *apocope*, which literally means 'cutting off'. You can see it in the dangling useless *b* of a tail trailing, dumbly, behind *lamb*, the silent *b* of a lame dumb lamb where *b* is a tuft of wool left on the wire once the flock's moved on, a ghost-marker. The word *apocope* comes from a different root to that of *apocalypse*, which is related to notions of 'disclosure'.

The thrown pyjamas get halfway to the spider then crumple in mid-air. They become floor and, in the same way that a black cat's yawn can cause a sudden new colour and potential violence to a scene, your crumpled silk pyjamas change the room entirely. They sprawl a glowing chalk outline on the carpet.

The spider responds to my inroads upon its personal space by making its life all about the word *akimbo*, attempting to spell it out with his anatomy. He seems proud in his great bulk. He is fat with his own silk, beckoning, and he is the whole point of this room now that you've gone. The spider and the silk pyjamas. I think I shall throw this paper-weight at him later.

The Brothers Grimm wrote a huge, popular dictionary that outsold all their famous monster tales – with its first edition reaching something like eight volumes it was far from itsy-bitsy. They wrote a fairy story that began 'A SPIDER and a FLEA dwelt together in one house, and brewed their beer in an egg-shell'. Since reading that at an impressionable age, I have always divided people into spiders and fleas. Something to do with one being willing to wait around, the other having its fill and leaving. I'll tidy this thought up later.

A whole hour of staring at a door thinking of the right word to say is certainly not the best way to spend one's time. For example, I could have boiled twenty eggs, contiguously. Purely to pass the time I finished the red wine that we had opened and then because it felt a pity to let go of the glass at this point I filled it with some Calvados that had been sitting in the back of the cupboard since Christmas. It struck me that the spider was also wasting its time just sitting there but this is, perhaps, uncharitable – it might be making a dream-catcher for me, attic of thought in intense, gossamer chaos. I try shouting at the spider by way of a trial run. It moves and I wonder whether it takes commissions – it could make a web, a network to span the gap that I could not cross by crawling. He is immune to his own glue, I imagine. Good little architect, his noun found somewhere between *spice* and *spigot*.

I try out some other choice words on him.

Even though it's dark, it occurs to me that noticing the spider must have been the prompt I needed and I leave the house to get rid of your abandoned silk pyjamas. It feels like there is an etiquette to be observed; you cannot just chuck silk pyjamas in a domestic bin that you have to live around. The council frowns on bonfires.

I looked it up later – in dire straits cobwebs can be compacted to make excellent DIY poultices that staunch blood. Sussex folklore recommends a dose of spiders in cases of jaundice, going as far as prescribing 'a live spider rolled up in butter'. But I am not marching all the way to Sussex. There must be a bin somewhere in London that is anonymous enough for your abandoned pyjamas.

'There's no prey here any more,' I said to the spider before I left, softly, silkily but with an edge, like those ribbons in the expensive books that we decided not to open in case it damages their spines.

Here's another spider-fact – there is a species in the Philippines that uses insect corpses and jungle debris to build spider-shaped decoys for its web. There was an accompanying quotation within the body of the article: 'One spider that had recently moulted integrated his shed skin into the decoy.'

I admit I did think about trapping the spider in that old *acetabula et calculi*/bait-and-switch/cup-and-postcard manoeuvre and chucking him out of a window, but the first cup I saw on the dresser – my wine glass, as I have mentioned, was busy with abandoned apple brandy – was the one you had given me last year, the purple one with *NO #1 GEEK* painted on it. I have always hated that mug but was too polite to ever tell you outright. The word *geek* had its first recorded use in 1919 and was defined with this quotation: 'A performer at a carnival or circus whose show consists of bizarre acts, such as biting the head off a live animal.' So I look up, I look further up, I feel like I am forever looking up at words, and references, up at spiders, and I read about Mike the Headless Chicken, the circus performer who died in 1947. He collapsed in a motel in Phoenix, Arizona – Mike the Headless Chicken has collapsed, oh get up Mike we love you, rise from Phoenix, please Mike.

> *Geek* also exists as a verb: 1. *intr.* To give up, to back down; to lose one's nerve.

It must have been fewer than two hours that I spent staring at the door that you slammed. I am now stomping somewhere around Bloomsbury and thinking that I could have roasted a fish on that glare you gave as you left. We had never fought before: such a thing would have seemed ludicrous and *row* would be a nonsense word. I would sooner expect a Hammond organ to replace your tongue. But it wasn't a row, not really, or at least had none of the smarting tingle or relief that rows allow. It was instead a slow, steady list of explanations. Clear and concise. You were always very clear and concise. I was the grumble and dissonance, you the perfect chord. So many of those obvious discrepancies – you silk, me wool from the lame dumb lamb, *fol de rol de trolmydame*, and here I am suddenly near the Mall thinking of all the work the un-butter-fed worms must have had to have put in so that you could have silk pyjamas to leave for me to throw at a spider.

Pure *esprit d'escalier*, this. Any words that come to me now which I *could* have said to you at the time are all false or imaginary friends. I could never stand the way you licked your thumb before you turned a page and I'm a little lost by an Opera House.

When London is late and undefined like this, when you imagine that lamps are being lit only to scorch the moths and the clouds make a candy-colour of the evening, the passers-by have conversations that marble together like endpapers. It's all beginnings and ends and plotless middles, boys and girls in doorways and bus stops, coats and boots the same colour as puddles and the pavements. One person there by the theatre – just there with the umbrella – they looked a bit like you as they passed but the spider and I could tell that the way you use vowels is entirely different, that the breeze coming through their just-open teeth made heavy with expectation of a – yawn? a yawp? a rejoinder? – is entirely different to any sound I have ever heard you make. You are *not* carrying an umbrella near me as I look for a place to throw away your pyjamas. Close call, though, and I'm still, obviously, a little lost for words because you were already through the door when a yarn unspooled somewhere inside me and rolled from the root of your tongue to your fingers on the door to the root of a word, finding the index of the book, the nervous-root of a bookmark that makes a book into a map, that networks me over, *wherever did you find these?*, silk, pursed, sow's, chaff, ear, the chaff re-burnt in the wander of the heat of the *said* and the solid golden meat of a goodbye, spider-fed, and I don't believe a word of it.

You had knocked on the bedroom door knowing that I would be at my desk, dreading absolutely nothing. No doubt I was busy performing all those actions that one makes with one's mouth when one doesn't realise one is being watched by a spider: chewing at a lip, working wine-smudges from the corner of my mouth, overusing the word *one* and frowning as if concertina'd brow-skin can juice ideas from brain to paper.

I remember when you threw a book at me. You had missed your mark and it fell out of the open window. I had remonstrated, we reconciled and we read somewhere that if a book gets wet we should freeze it and that a domestic fridge will be fine for this if in a pinch: 'If possible freeze the book spine down, and supported so it won't lean or fall over.'

All that editing and book-throwing and yet I still did not have the right thing to say before the door shut behind you.

A tip for users (Easy): when working out the right word to shout at a departing figure, remember Hell is other people and is cognate with Old Frisian *helle* or *hille*. In Norse myth the goddess Hel rides in a boat made from dead men's fingernails.

A tip for users (Intermediary): when working out the right word to shout at a departing figure, concentrate on tone. This is applicable at any time of the day – whether a Calvados-scented, unrealised, uncharitable harnessing of a moon-quiver or a sunslice, a hot and unpalatable word that puts too much emphasis on vowels and the parting of a mouth and the opening of a window through which a book or pyjamas can be thrown might be too much, as might a breath silver and polished newly-convex in the water, or a pigeon's parentheses of wings, or nape-shots, shots of coffee that I'd bring to you one morning, or a deviation of form from a set or acceptable path, or a chicanery of purpose or a resettling of livery, a duck, ill-liveried and fingerless; this is a way of saying that a duck is chuckling darkly in the London park where traditionally spies meet as I toddle drunkenly around the capital still searching for a bin.

I know what the tense future holds. I know that I'll be heckling the spider for days and pretending it is you, *esprit d'escalier*, the spy that watches the staircase. He'll seem appreciative of the discourse and he might waggle appreciatively.

A tip for beginners: spiders are not great conversationalists. There is the understanding that they do not have *this* – a fingerprint that touches your face, that conveys so much electricity and so much inelastic blood and bone that it is not much more than re-compacted chalk. Maybe I'll say something obscene to the spider, and with the unspellable pressure of eight legs winching in on themselves, the slow scud of disapproval, each of the spider's legs will bend forward as he laughs at me, each leg in exactly the same position as the Anglepoise lamp on my desk.

The entomology-etymology puns are obvious. The word *insect* comes from 'that which is cut in pieces or engraved/segmented'. See *bisect*. See: *broken-up*. See: *What's the difference between a* bisect *and a* rebuffed hello? See: *but you do know that a spider isn't an insect, don't you?* Now, that could be a door opening, a window opening, a door closing, a mouth opening. Big Sam Johnson tells us a tarantula is an 'an insect whose bite is cured only by music'. Words words words on the page, give me excess of them crabbed and spidery, but as I tried to say the right word to check you at the bedroom door I found that they were a mouthful of wasps – dead, with the sting removed. It should be action instead – I should punch the moon from its purchase in order that I might serve you tea upon it, and other glib, active idioms I've just created because the language I should have had at my fingertips was just some kind of soft and unpleasantly buckled mirror, hazy with unexpected marks and useless words.

When all my words are boiled down, frozen, re-dried: without you, London is just 1) *n.* the angle between this lamp-post and this brick wall's ivy, and all its angled heads, probably filled with spiders 2) *n.* this nameless street 3) *n.* this rubbish bin there, where I feed your silks.

A tip for users: when working out the right word to shout at a departing figure, be carried away in the truthlessness of definition. Ours was a sprained sky, and birds sparked out from the new-bent joist of it. Be Headless Mike in Phoenix. Be the dumb lame lamb. Weave your new network, toss and turn, and spin it out.

Acknowledgements

Versions of some of these stories first appeared in journals including *3:AM Magazine*, *Ambit*, *Belleville Park Pages*, *Hotel*, *The Lonely Crowd*, *Night&Day*, *Structo*, *Visual Verse* and *The White Review*. 'Mischief' was commissioned by Wales Arts Review for their Story|Retold series, responding to the work of Frank Richards. Lyrics for 'I'd Do Anything' taken from Lionel Bart's musical *Oliver!* (1960).

Too many people enabled this collection. In an attempt to spread the blame, however: thank you Fiona and Catherine Williams for being *squinch* and *superstructure* and always showing me whales' heartstrings. I am grateful to Prudence Chamberlain, Špela Drnovšek Zorko and Nisha Ramayya for their ever-illuminating conversations and for illuminating generally. Thank you Olivia Raglan, Jenny Selvakumaran, Victoria Schindler and Rachel Lambert! Thanks, Robert Weedon, and to all involved with *purpureus* and *Generative Constraints*.

I am much obliged to Judith Hawley, Kristen Kreider and Andrew Motion at Royal Holloway, University of London and to my students there – you inspire the best in me and will be able to pick apart this whole business very skillfully. Sincere gratitude to Preti Taneja, Rebecca Prestwood and Declan Ryan, Rose McNamee, Annabel Banks, Matt Lomas, and to Joanna Walsh and Nick Murray for their early encouragements. Sarah Gulick, Christina McLeish, Sarah Phelps, Marika Prokosh, Olivia Potts, Ella Risbridger, Anna Scott, Emma Southon, Isabella Streffen, Alice Tarbuck, Kate Young, Fiona Zublin and their various Difficult associates – thank you all for your company and for your shoulders.

Thanks Kit Caless, Gary Budden and Sanya Semakula for taking a punt out on a limb for me, and other mixed metaphors. Thank you Lucy Luck, for your patience and providence, and to Kishani Widyaratna and the whole team at 4th Estate for new berths and livery.